ANGELO

JEAN GIONO (1895–1970) was born in Manosque, Provence, the son of an Italian cobbler, and lived there most of his life. He supported his family working as a bank clerk for eighteen years (with an interval serving in the ranks in the First World War) before his first two novels were published, thanks to the generosity of André Gide, to critical acclaim. He went on to write thirty novels and numerous essays and stories, as well as poetry and plays. In 1953 he was awarded the Prix Monégasque for his collective work. The same year, he made a prescient contribution to the "ecological" movement with his novella *The Man who Planted Trees*. This, and his novel *The Horseman on the Roof*, which was made into a highly-acclaimed film starring Olivier Martinez and Juliette Binoche, are also published by Harvill. Jean Giono married in 1920 and had two daughters.

Angelo is the first of a group of four novels all featuring the same cavalry-officer hero. It was not the first to be written: having completed the three others, *Mort d'un personnage*, *Le Hussard sur le toit (The Horseman on the Roof)*, and *Le Bonheur fou*, the author returned to his sketch for *Le Hussard sur le toit* and fleshed it out to provide the hero with a previous history.

Jean Giono

ANGELO

*Translated from the French
by A. E. Murch*

THE HARVILL PRESS
LONDON

First published with the title *Angelo* by Editions Gallimard, Paris, 1958
First published in Great Britain in 1960 by Peter Owen Ltd

This edition first published in 1998 by
The Harvill Press,
84 Thornhill Road,
London N1 1RD

1 3 5 7 9 8 6 4 2

Copyright © Editions Gallimard, 1958
English translation copyright © Peter Owen Ltd, 1960

A CIP catalogue record for this book is available from the British Library

ISBN 1 86046 024 0

Designed and typeset in Bembo at
Libanus Press, Marlborough, Wiltshire

Printed and bound in Great Britain by Butler & Tanner Ltd
at Selwood Printing, Burgess Hill

AUTHOR'S PREFACE

Angelo is not a sequel to *Le Bonheur fou*; rather is it the opening of an early draft of *Le Hussard sur le toit*, written in 1934, and shows Angelo leaving Turin, settling in Aix-en-Provence and meeting Pauline before the outbreak of the cholera epidemic. It is a preliminary presentation of the *dramatis personae*.

The hero, Angelo, sprang to life in Marseilles on the pavement outside the Home for Reformed Prostitutes. At that time I was spending a few months with my friends the Pelous, who lived at the far end of the Boulevard Baille, now called the Rue Yves-Lariven. I was given "Mémée's room", which overlooked the playground of a nursery school. Beyond lay the grounds of the Timone lunatic asylum, then the railway tracks of La Blancarde where I could hear the expresses roaring past at night. It was a filthy winter, and the train whistles, scattered by the squally gusts, sounded as brave as the horns in Mozart. As I lay half asleep and beautifully snug (the ideal state for a historian), I would listen to the trains as they rushed at top speed towards Aubagne, brandishing their whistling sabres.

Every day I used to walk past the Home for Reformed Prostitutes; as I followed its boundary wall I took fresh delight in the crests of the cedars and cypresses that overtopped its height of a good twenty feet. Mémée, whose room I occupied, told me that behind this wall was a garden where a hound was set loose at night to prevent the escape of any girls who had not reformed sufficiently, a matter that gave me plenty of food for thought.

The façade of this building flaunted its name in Gothic characters made of cement, and fronted the boulevard between a police station and a bicycle repair shop. That is where, one evening, Angelo was born. While passing the police station I had not even thought of him; in front of the bicycle shop he was on horseback; and by the time I reached home he already had a past. (The Police Commissioner from Turin came straight out of that police station on the Boulevard Baille, traces of his origin sticking to him like scraps of eggshell on the down of a chick.)

I began to write down this past of his in "Mémée's room". It was not a question of writing a novel, but of drawing up a memorandum that might eventually be of service to me when writing a novel. *Angelo* was written during those months, while, all through the stormy nights between, the express trains swept past with their flourish of trumpets. *The Horseman on the Roof*, a work of very different calibre, kept me busy for eight years. This time, though, it was simply a question of analysing this new-born character and testing the elements revealed by that analysis. To break down this composition into its component parts (not forgetting its background of howling gales and whistling trains), the appropriate reagent seemed to be a woman. First I introduced Anna Clèves: the reaction she produced led me to bring in a second, Pauline de Théus.

This text is therefore a simple laboratory report, jotted down even while the experiment was proceeding. Above everything I wanted to see how my hero would respond to a given set of circumstances. I was not composing, but experimenting. That is why Angelo does not, in this book, come to grips with any widely shared emotion as he does in the cholera epidemic described in the sequel. His heart is stirred by nothing more than the love of women, in particular of Pauline de Théus. To bring about her dramatic entrance, torch in hand, in the darkness of a house beset by the plague, called for the skill of a novelist, not of a mere dabbler, and this was the task of the years that followed.

The reader will notice (in addition to any actual errors I may have made), that I have allowed myself a certain latitude in the apparatus of my experiment, that is to say in the invention of facts. First, the egg with a portrait of Napoleon on its shell; this egg was mentioned by Stendhal, I no longer recall exactly where, but I am positive it is there.* Next, it will be possible to discover a sort of similarity between Angelo's situation in Aix-en-Provence and that of Lucien Leuwen at Nancy (particularly in respect of the gamekeeper). Finally, I make Angelo whistle a Brahms waltz that did not exist at that period, 1832 – Brahms was born in 1833.

---

*Among some miscellaneous items that Stendhal probably collected from a newspaper I have managed to find the passage he mentions about an egg marked with Napoleon's head. This brief text is entitled: *Sur la Province française. 1. La Poule (Cons. d'octobre 1816):* "I come to a village where everyone is talking of a hen that has laid an egg flattened on one side. On the flat part was a clear outline of a 5 franc piece showing the head. (They prudently did not specify that it was Napoleon's.)" . . . "After 5 or 6 days the local authority sent gendarmes to arrest the poultry-woman, her husband, the egg and the hen. The hen died in prison. The others were released a fortnight later." (*Mélanges de Littérature*, Divan, vol. II, p. 183–184.)

ANGELO

I

CAVOUR, THAT CHARMING FELLOW of the auburn side whiskers, had not yet begun to sing his songs in praise of political freedom, when secret societies were already chanting the swelling themes of an *opera seria* inspired by the same love of liberty in the forests of the Kingdom of Piedmont.

Supporters of the *carbonari* came from all classes of society. Aristocrats, artisans, officers, sailors, teachers, soldiers, students, even impetuous women schooled to discretion by the thrilling risks of this romantic political movement, all banded together to form a shadowy fraternity that regarded courage and fidelity to one's oath as sacred.

The dangers they faced were prodigious. Though cloudless blue skies evoke sympathy for liberal ideals, and the kingdom basked in that Mediterranean warmth which takes an affectionate view of political assassination, the authorities were obliged to shoot the well-meaning assassins with elaborate salutes but pretty wicked Sardinian bullets. The nerves of the Austrian monarchy could not endure the loss of even the most insignificant of her spies, but she solaced her alarm and despondency with forty divisions of well-built grenadiers.

One May morning in 18–, the body of a certain Baron Schwartz, a native of Lombardy by his own account, was discovered under some bushes two leagues from Turin. He had openly been in the pay of Spielberg, and only a short time before had denounced three cobblers who were allegedly plotting together as they sat stitching their welts. As soon as his death was known, a little ballad, obviously composed beforehand, was being sung everywhere in the streets of Turin, bluntly suggesting that the Baron must have offended someone who was particularly interested in boots. But the police gave every sign of taking the matter seriously.

The corpse was bare to the waist and his breast, white as a woman's, was all streaked with trickles of dried sweat. The late Baron still clutched in his right hand the hilt of a sabre, and clearly this was no make-believe duel, for he had fought hard and long in defence of his life. His only wound, the one that killed him, could scarcely have been made by a sword, which in the heat of a fight always lacerates the flesh a little. This blow, precise as a rapier thrust, had been struck by a pointed weapon that adroitly pierced the heart.

There was at that time in Turin a police Commissioner who knew a little about swordsmanship, and this wound seemed to him highly suggestive. "A stroke like that," said he, "needs ten years of practice and three hundred years of hereditary aptitude." This official was, moreover, a man of keen intelligence – under a pseudonym he wrote short novels of character which possessed some literary value – and he gave considerable attention to a psychological fact. All the evidence in this case showed that the man who killed the Baron had not only scorned to stab him in the back, but had been magnanimous enough to allow him to defend himself! A hardened blackguard like Schwartz! Only one man was capable of such monumental generosity! Alas! There could be no doubt of his identity. Schwartz was not the only spy in the town – far from it! – and in a couple of days the Austrian Chancellery would probably announce the name of the culprit with the usual ironical comments.

"Irony will ever be the weapon of the weaker party," sighed the Commissioner. The whole town applauded his naiveté in sending eight police constables in all their glory (three would have been plenty), to the Pardi Palace at about five o'clock that afternoon. He had no need to recommend them to make as much noise as they could – such an instruction would have considerably puzzled their simple minds – and with their great boots they were bound to wake the echoes in the narrow cobbled alleys that twist around the palace before leading out into the market place. There these guileless fellows asked the porter to take them to Colonel Angelo of the Hussars. (He was the natural son of that tender-hearted, passionate Duchess, Ezzia Pardi, a very lanky young man of twenty-five, with thin lips and beautiful black velvet eyes.) The porter replied that His Lordship had unfortunately gone out only half an hour before the arrival of his eight distinguished visitors. An orderly, lolling about in the courtyard, kindly added the information that the Colonel had gone visiting, very probably to call upon a lady, for he was wearing full-dress uniform and riding his charger. Whereupon the eight shovel-hatted gendarmes exchanged a wink or two and settled themselves in the palace entrance hall to smoke their malodorous little black cigars and wait for Angelo's return.

Two days later, a French customs officer, taking an evening stroll to stretch his legs outside the frontier post on the road from Italy to Mont Genèvre, looked towards Cesana and saw a rider approaching, as erect as an ear of golden corn and mounted on a black horse. Looking closer, he recognised him for an officer of the King of Sardinia's Hussars in full uniform, coming at a walking pace. The Piedmont customs house is lower down, out of sight beyond a turn in the road, and the horseman was thus already on French soil, riding forward with perfect non-chalance as he achieved his invasion.

The weather was full of that promise of spring which can so readily lead a man to make foolhardy decisions, especially at this altitude and at twilight. The customs officer had just finished his supper of raw onions in the guardhouse, and something about this elegant horseman irritated him so much that he cocked his gun. The rider was daydreaming, idly fingering his reins, while his epaulettes and gold braid glistened like oil with every movement of his horse. The guard felt that such absent-mindedness was particularly insolent. "This fine fellow," he thought to himself, "seems altogether too off-hand, strolling into France as though it belonged to him! I'll soon put a stop to that, and show him the sort of man I am!" Yet in spite of himself he was fascinated by the arabesques and trefoils of gold braid that covered the rider's cloak, by his golden helmet with its tossing plumes. Below the helmet the guard began to make out the rider's face, strangely noble and grave, while his thoughts ran on: "The most I can lose is that instead of a silver crown he'll toss me a few stumps from his cigar-case when I send him back the way he came."

He was standing beside a barricade like a sheep-hurdle but more than six feet high, placed across the road to mark where fortified French territory began. The rider, still with his air of dreamy unconcern, was now only four yards from the guard's pistol, which was levelled in full view. Suddenly, by some magical impetus that sprang from his leg muscles (or primarily from his heart, as the Duchess Ezzia would have said, had she been there with her romantic memories), he made his horse crouch like a cat and spring effortlessly over the barrier. The customs man, utterly astounded by the rider's calm audacity and by the mournful smile that flickered over his thin lips as he sailed past, hardly had time to mutter, "That highwayman will make me lose my twelve sous a day!" and fire his pistol in the air before the horseman was galloping out of sight into the forests that cascade down towards the French valleys.

Later that same night, towards two o'clock in the morning, the landlord of *The Maltese Cross* in Briançon climbed upstairs to wake a horsedealer from Monetier who was staying at the inn for St Mary's Fair, and made him creep down barefoot to the stable to examine, out of sight of any prying eyes, a black horse that stood there trembling and wretched. "I bought him a few hours ago," he explained, "and he won't touch his oats." The dealer turned up a hoof, saw the brand of the Royal Cavalry on the iron horseshoe, and blandly asked where the rider's uniform was. It was brought to him from a corn-bin, and the moment he saw that it belonged to a colonel he swore by all his gods that he would have nothing to do with the affair. There was something behind this that was sure to mean trouble. Besides, in his opinion, the animal was so fine, so sensitive, that already it was pining and would undoubtedly die of grief at being separated from its master. In the end, putting a good face on his offer, he volunteered to take the risk of buying the horse for three crowns, after he had been assured that the Colonel had bartered his uniform for a navvy's old suit of white corduroy and left the town hours ago by the Embrun Gate.

Angelo had, in fact, lost no time in putting the walls of the fortress behind him. To avoid the patrols he kept at a good distance from the main road, walking through the osier beds and thickets of alder that fringe the banks of the Durance. He was thoroughly enjoying the physical pleasure of wearing clothes that were too large for him, and the cuffs of his long sleeves, rubbing against the backs of his hands, reminded him with every step he took that he must play out this game of brazen bluff to the end, mastering hidden threats as Italian hearts love to do. The moon showed him the way through pine forests and safely past isolated cottages, which he negotiated with smooth duplicity. He had retained a beautifully wrought dagger, and could feel it weighing down the inside pocket of his jacket. His spirits soared to a mood of high exaltation as he said to himself: "Here I am in the birthplace of Freedom," and he watched the dawn flaunt its colours like a peacock's tail above the mountains.

All day he walked, never stopping to rest or to ask for food, though along footpaths near farms or villages he met country girls who gave him sympathetic glances. His own eyes, though he was quite unaware of it, shone with the light of eager love. "The teachings of Voltaire and Montesquieu are in the very air one breathes in this place," he said to himself. "In Montezemollo, the poorest yokel must gamble for his life and the bread of his wife and children against the little black spy that walks through his fields in a cassock. Their complete subjection to the Church may make our Italian peasants more cunning that those who live here, but whenever I come across any of them by a hedgerow they destroy my faith in the sublime. Yet, unless I can believe that noble souls may dwell in the simplest of men, how can I preserve my own integrity and keep my zest for living?"

In the evening he went quietly through Embrun, where for three sous he bought a small white cheese and half a loaf still warm from the oven, and ventured to speak to a labourer's wife beating some scraps of cloth outside her door. She stayed silent a moment, her eyes on his grave, sensitive face. Peasant woman as she was, she was perceptive enough to know she had no cause to be alarmed at the magnificent sweep of his wide felt hat as he bowed to her, or at his flashing eyes and the passionate urgency in his voice as he ended by asking her where the Royal Stagecoach started.

"Stop making sheep's eyes," she said, "and don't raise your hat so much unless your pockets are empty." To see him so fine and handsome, yet so frank and unassuming, gave her a twinge of irritation. He thought to himself: "This simple woman has seen right through me. I must have blood on my hands, like Macbeth. I had better give her an explanation she can understand. This morning," he continued aloud, "I was going to run away with my master's daughter. She loves me and I have promised to marry her. I was in her room, helping her to pack the things she would need. When I jumped out of the window, her brother, a great lout of a fellow who hates her because she is older than him, tried to kill me with a cudgel. I defended myself and wounded him in the thigh with my knife. I managed to send word to the girl I regard as my wife that I would wait for her in the courtyard where the Royal Stagecoach starts, but since we lived out in the country and I've never come into town before, I don't know where they run from and am trying to find out. That's why I doubtless look rather distracted."

As he told her this tale his modest tone of voice made him doubly attractive. "But the Royal Stagecoaches run from Gap, child," she replied kindly. "Does your ladylove know that?" "I'm sure she does. She is the daughter of a farmer who lives two leagues from here," he answered, wondering to himself: "Why does this good woman call me 'child'? I'm six foot tall and I terrify the recruits of the King's Hussars!"

"Then you'll have to move quickly," the woman went on. "I hope your legs are good, for you've sixteen leagues to go. All you have to do is walk like a local man, as unconcerned as if you lived here, go past the police station you see down there, behind the big elm where the gendarme is smoking his pipe. Take the first road on your right and you will not need to cross the bridge, that is always guarded at night." After she had told him with much animation and copious detail exactly where the coaching stage was at Gap, he sauntered on, indulging his whim by brushing against the legs of the gendarme who sat smoking his pipe.

Scarcely had he turned the corner she had spoken of when he heard someone calling. It was the woman again, her skirts billowing out as she ran. "Haven't you got a passport?" she panted, all out of breath. "No," he replied. "That's what I thought. Here! Take this! It's the identity book of a tailor's assistant who used to live with us. He forgot to take it when he left. He was not as tall as you," she went on, lowering her head a little, "but a gendarme won't notice any difference, especially at night. If they question you, stick to it that you worked for Mme Thérèse. That is, if it suits you to," she added with a flush of embarrassment, crumpling the hem of her apron. He took both her hands in his to thank her, feeling his good luck was at its peak. "What grand people these are!" he mused as he walked on with great strides.

He covered some two leagues of the cross-country road while dusk was falling, and luckily forded the Durance with the last vestige of daylight. When he gained the high road, night had fallen. He passed through a village where he saw no sign of life. The only lamp in the main street shone on the brass plate of a notary, and Angelo, light-hearted enough to give rein to a fanciful conceit, thought to himself: "Perhaps inside that house there lives an old student of historical curiosities. The lion and arrow on the seal of my ring would mean a good deal to him."

Dogs were barking in distant farms, the sound giving depth and perspective to a dreamlike countryside where meadows lay white as milk and the almost transparent ghosts of trees stood decked with moonlight. He was still thinking of his ring. "By wearing it I risk drawing upon myself the derision that these sarcastic people keep specially for those sons of the Church who fail to maintain their prerogatives. It is fortunate that the open-hearted freedom-loving woman who helped me just now did not notice it. If she had, there would have been no more frankness. From now on I must keep my wits about me."

On he went, mile after mile, through this darkened countryside where the nearness of the forests and the overhanging mountains lent an atmosphere of brooding tragedy, thinking of the dangers his impetuous spirit might bring upon him. "I never know how to respond to banter, or, rather, I know only one way to reply," and he fingered the dagger in his pocket. "What a pity it would be to kill one of those worthy men who went mad with excitement when they managed to acquire a political constitution. I cannot take anything lightly. For me, every-thing is serious. For them, nothing is important; they would sell their homeland for the fun of turning a witty phrase or giving point to a joke. Can they, I wonder, still feel enthusiasm for noble ideals? Are they any longer capable of fervour, or has their habit of sarcasm killed all their finer feelings?" He grew conscious of weariness, and felt so bitter that he even wondered whether he ought to have tipped the woman who had given him the workman's identity book.

He had just passed a crossroads when he saw the light of a lantern behind him. Shortly after, he heard horses trotting and the noise of wheels. "In any case," said he, "these people, whoever they are, will not dare to poke fun at me. I should imagine there won't be any question of irony at this time of night, and in this lonely stretch of country. I'll ask them whether I'm still on the right road for that town where the stagecoach starts." He stood in the middle of the road as the carriage came up to him, a small but cumbersome vehicle. The man driving it reined in his horses and thrust his hand in his pocket. "Get out of the way, you brigand," he shouted.

"Don't be alarmed," said Angelo, stepping forward into the light of the carriage-lamp. "I only want to ask . . ."

"What is the matter?" a woman's voice called, clear and firm.

"In a moment there will be no matter, Madame la Marquise," returned the driver. At the same instant the window of the carriage door was lowered, and Angelo saw the outline of a large lace cap.

"Why, it's a child!" she exclaimed. "Dominique, didn't you notice he's only a child? Come here, my boy."

"I do apologise, Madame, . . ."

". . . and a well brought-up child, too," she went on. "His accent reminds me a little of Piedmont. But what do you want, my lad?"

Angelo made his enquiry, courteously expressing his regret if he had caused alarm. "You haven't frightened anyone," the lady assured him, "except Dominique. That's all." She rapped on a panel with the handle of her cane. "Have you lost your nerve, Dominique? Shall we have to treat you like a timid horse, and make you put your nose against the shadow that scared you? Can you see now that he's just a child?"

The man in the box-seat was a giant with huge shoulders. "Saving your presence, Madame," said he, "I don't like children who roam about at midnight."

"Well, I do," the voice retorted. "So you are on your way to the stagecoach? Get in, then, my boy." The door opened, a little step tumbled forward, and Angelo recovered his social graces sufficiently to step elegantly over enormous skirts.

"I am an old woman," the voice came again, "so it's pointless to tire yourself with gallantries. If you feel drowsy, go to sleep."

2

"THE MARQUISE CÉLINE DE THÉUS is a liberal," the Prefect of Gap was wont to exclaim, and then he would stamp up and down so fiercely in his tightly strapped trousers that the spring under his instep twanged like a guitar. On special occasions he would even add: "She's a liberal with a vengeance." But after daring to express his views in such forthright terms he would stalk rapidly off to join some group or other on the far side of the room, for in point of fact he was terrified of that serene and vigorous old lady. The truth is that she had no use for the artificial phrases and gestures of high society: she had all the simplicity of an egg. "But," Baron d'Avêne would say, "it is extremely disagreeable to have an egg smashed against your shirt front."

Her evergreen integrity, allied with a voice powerful enough to shatter Bohemian crystal, made it possible for her to petrify the most blasé assembly with a couple of words, and in the breathless hush that followed she would go on breathing serenely, her eyes as innocent as daisies, unscathed, and as ready as a bull to charge again. She thus had the gift of laying bare, as though with a pickaxe, those secret places of the heart where salamanders lay hibernating, their inner fires scorching even the very attire of the men and women who harboured them. After one of her blunt quips, how many of her hearers felt the same swift urge to cover themselves that Adam and Eve knew after the Fall! "What is the use of having fifty thousand silk weavers working for me in Lyons," protested little Mme de Gaucourt, "if I am to lie sobbing all the morning in my satin bed, as I've done every day this week? How can any of you endure the things she says?" There was no one who could. "Au revoir, my friends," the old Marquise would say roundly, leaving behind her a room full of people, all choking over one of those home truths that ruthlessly unmask the hypocrisies of statecraft, family life or the human heart.

But after such strokes as these, the woman whom Dominique drove home to the castle of Théus would bury herself in a corner of her clumsy little carriage, the reflection of the countryside flickering over her sad, unfathomable eyes as in an invisible mirror. At a rapid trot her homeward journey took two hours, first through meadow land along a winding road bordered with poplars, then across open country, among high bare tawny hills. After climbing these barren slopes the road crossed a drawbridge that could no longer be raised, and ran straight into the courtyard. The chateau dominated the valley and commanded a thousand square leagues of Alpine peaks, black, silent and tumultuous.

The Marquise entered the hall and laid her head-dress on a side table. Her thick hair was grey and straight. She moved three steps to the left, halting before a great portrait of a man, strikingly virile and with a most commanding presence, painted in enamelled colours. It was the forward surge of his body, amazing in its grace, that first monopolised one's interest; only later, and because a brightness drew one's eye upward, did one notice his face. It was rather full; his blond moustache twirled into two little sharp curved points; his soft brown eyes almost level with his huge fleecy black wig.

"Well, Diablon?" the Marquise would say, and seemed to listen for some time to an answer from the painted lips. Then, with bent head, she would climb the wide staircase and walk along a corridor that seemed endless, her footsteps echoing strangely in the emptiness.

She lived on the first floor in the staterooms. Three great salons, each amply large enough for a ball, stretched one beyond the other, connected by wide folding doors now thrown open to their fullest extent. A vast array of tall Venetian mirrors, chandeliers with myriads of crystal drops, huge glass-fronted cabinets, all reflected one another, multiplying the expanse of these rooms, and their loneliness. The faintest ray of light created an infinite sequence of tiny, distant rainbows like a cloud of iridescent molecules sparking from wall to wall. Everything was wonderfully neat and clean. The bare wood of the parquet floor shone with wax. On side tables whole services of fine crystal goblets were set out as though in perpetual readiness for some ghostly carousal, and in the silence the faintest breath of warm air was enough to set them tinkling faintly. Every evening, as soon as it was dusk, lights gleamed from the candelabras, sconces, lustres and candlesticks. Then, above the light sounds made by the crystal came the quiet, velvety hum of wax candles with their little spurting flames.

In the most northerly corner of this icy vista, overwhelming as it was to mind and spirit, the Marquise had had placed the gilded box of a sedan chair. This she finally entered, settled herself on its cushioned seat, spread out her skirts, placed her old hands flat on her thighs and went back in thought to the days when she was young.

In those days she had had cheeks like rosy apples and the robust health of an outdoor life. Born of this mountain country, she had the natural birthright of a heart purer than the spring water whose freshness she could still taste on her lips. She had never been beautiful, not even pretty, but "I had that same freshness," she would say.

Her father ruled at Théus in those days, undisputed master of the mountains and plains, the woodcutters and harvesters, a splendid figure of a man, who wore his thick hair unpowdered (save by the passing years), whose fair skin was still smooth as a rose petal. Tall and spare, always clad in a jacket of supple calf-skin and leather gaiters that reached his knees, leaping from crag to crag with the stride of a Wandering Jew, waving his arms like a windmill to keep his balance, he was a familiar sight as he busied himself with his estates from one year's end to another, selling the timber of his immense forests to the royal shipyards at Toulon. Some of his trees, the tallest and straightest – as was only right – went out as masts crowded with sail and carrying the royal ensign to the far side of the ocean. Already he, too, lived a lonely life, for his wife had died five years after the birth of their second child, their daughter. Sometimes, when he could no longer endure the pangs of solitude, he would cry out for feasting and revelry, summon his valets, order horses to be saddled and send couriers far and wide. A ruthless onslaught played havoc with his choicest poultry, the finest beasts in his herds, the treasures of his cellar, and, seething with dark fervour, he would array himself slowly and with infinite care in satin, silks and fine gold, powder and per-fumes that little Céline would come and spray over him, standing on tiptoe to reach his face. Then the salons, vast though they were, were yet too small to contain all the local nobility who flocked to enjoy these luscious feasts which were always planned with a devilish love of excess and such supreme elegance that the effect was overpowering. It was enough to bring on the vapours (and on each occasion ladies swooned from this cause alone) if one chanced to look through the wide-open windows at the silent, threat-ening wilderness outside when one's heart was already lulled with music and tender feelings.

It was in these ballrooms, on one such night, that Céline saw Pierre de B. for the first time. What first caught her eye was the amazing buoyancy of his bodily movements, and it was some time before she glanced higher at the brightness of his face and his little pointed moustaches à la Turenne. "He was a very handsome man, very good, very tender, very fickle, yet at bottom very faithful," she would say aloud in the silence of the gilded box of her sedan chair. "Very faithful!" She looked down through the immeasurable emptiness of the deserted salons, and there, at the far end, he appeared before her eyes like a vision, so immense that his wig brushed the cream panels of the ceiling; his pumps slid over the parquet floor like Venetian gondolas; his white-clad leg poised forward like a mast swaying with the movement of the sea; his gentle brown eyes more brimming over with sorrow and love than a painting of heaven on Good Friday. The old Marquise closed her eyes and sighed.

During the forty years and more she had lived alone she saw every day, and every hour of the day, the spectre of the great body and twisted little soul of Pierre de B. She searched within herself for reasons to excuse his life and his death, and managed to find some; but, just as a little trickle of running water will seep up through the sand with which one tries to cover it, so his innate vulgarity could not be concealed by her daily effort for more than forty years. Then she gave up seeking excuses and did better: she continued to love him. She lived in the beau monde; she never ceased to keep open house; she therefore understood very well the inner workings, the mainspring and mechanism of his knaveries, and in the end she even came to appreciate some of the finer points; the cunning logic, the precise calculation of risk and advantage shown in some of his more brilliant coups, a game with singlesticks that demanded almost as much finesse as swordplay, of which she was a good judge. To herself she said that her Pierre was a prodigious fencer in his own type of combat. Though she served as a butt for every stroke he made, she alone knew that she was not a figure stuffed with straw, but a woman whose warm flesh, whose inmost being, was lacerated each time he struck. Yet, and again she was the only one to know it, she had a thousand hands ready to staunch those wounds instantly. No one had ever seen her bleed. Long ago, even while her Pierre was still alive, she ended by resolving that nothing of his passage at arms with the world at large should be allowed to affect her love for him. Though she profoundly despised herself for this decision, she made it, she kept it, she would always abide by it with the abysmal self-indulgence that nothing in heaven or earth can shake. She hated herself, yet believed that was better than hating the one she loved; she scorned herself, but felt the same certainty that it was better so. Then she would spend long hours in her sedan chair, thinking out complicated ways to bind up her wounds. Often, in spite of all her care, the dressings would slip when she was out in society, but she knew it, she was prepared for it, and she immediately had the presence of mind to snap savagely at handsome men and lovely women so that she could secretly lick her own wounds while they were openly licking theirs.

Pierre de B. had not been a great criminal, a fallen angel. If he had, Céline would gladly have gone with him to the palaces of the underworld, singing his praises all the way. No, on the contrary he had lived meanly (by fashionable standards), and had no ambition to improve. The little red-faced girl, as he called her, was for him first and last nothing more than a very rich heiress. Being accustomed to success with the ladies, he did not fail to notice the powerful impression he had made on her, and took full advantage of it. It was nothing to him that every time he went to Théus he came, as it seemed to her, out of the clouds like some fabulous horseman of the Apocalypse, sweeping away the only world this open-hearted child had ever known and building around her a verdant paradise of love. He was simply negotiating a good business deal in a way he thought perfectly natural. His most rapturous moment in the whole affair was when the notaries discussed the settlement of her fortune, and he saw coming within his grasp the broad estates, the immense stands of timber, the hard cash; wealth that would enable him to live as he chose. The little red-faced girl herself was merely an unavoidable encumbrance. After the wedding he carried her off to Paris with the rest of his luggage.

The day the marriage contracts were signed, Pierre de B. knew a moment of terror, and so experienced as much emotion as a man of his realistic nature could, when he at last came to know Laurent de Théus, Céline's elder brother. Chattering about him one day, she had said to Pierre: "He likes whipping tops." "What?" asked Pierre, stupidly enough, "does he really play with tops? I thought he was older than you." "He is ten years older than I am," she replied, "and he plays tops with men. You know the little wooden tops that one whips till they hum? That's what he does with men. He whips them till they yell in real earnest. He always has scores of men around, all terrified to death of him, and he's extraordinarily clever at orchestrating all their howls, a real virtuoso."

Laurent de Théus was thin and wiry like his father; he neither wore a wig nor powdered his hair, which was cut short in military fashion; his clothes were sumptuous in their restraint, their attention to detail; his linen and the lace at his throat and wrists were white as milk. Some secret aid to a strange conceit had given his face deep wrinkles and a sulphur-coloured scar that ran across his right cheek. This wound had affected the corner of his eye, keeping it half shut like the eye of a cat on the watch. He listened in silence as the service was read. He had not been presented to anyone nor did he introduce himself. He simply sat there like a block of ice. When it was over he rose and kissed his sister's hand. "Your tender heart was upsetting all my theories, my little rat," he said loudly. "How could I feel free to do as I liked in the face of such artlessness as yours? Your husband is a blackguard. I am delighted with this marriage. Now things will be evened up." So he took his leave, after standing pensive for a moment, knocking the dust from the back of his chair with the end of his gloves.

Pierre de B. was not a blackguard. He was a sensualist, obviously only of minor calibre, but a perfect specimen of the type. He took his pleasures wherever he could. He was an adept in self-gratification, and if, while taking his own pleasure, he occasionally gave pleasure to others, that was merely incidental. There was no devilry about him. On the contrary, he fostered his desires as an indulgent father does his children, quietly but thoroughly. Only Céline, with her amazing guilelessness, could have thought of calling him 'Diablon' as she did, moved by ecstasy or terror and completely submissive to his will. From their earliest days together he managed to avoid any difficulty with her. Financial difficulties, naturally, did not arise, and on the emotional side he was sufficiently expert to have nothing to fear.

He had not only a veritable deer-park of fine ladies, thanks to his god-like fascination, but also plenty of cocottes from the Rue de la Bûcherie or the maze of streets round Notre Dame, thanks to the money bags from Théus. So he could satisfy his highest aspirations. Nothing bewitched him more than the rounded limbs and tiny feet that are to be found only among the lower orders. He had to have them charmingly shod and meticulously sheathed in silk, luxuries that he provided. He also loved the pallid languor of high-born ladies, their airs and graces, their sighs and vapours, all their parade of fragility, for, in spite of his own swaggering display of strength, he was by no means sure that he was really strong.

Somewhat discountenanced by all these escapades which her husband made no pretence of concealing, Céline did her best to win him with her dog-like devotion. "Elegance," she once said to him, "is simply good health." (She believed that elegance appealed to him.) "Would you call your own thick throat elegant, or even healthy?" he retorted. "Your skin, Céline, is as rough as a tanner's rasp. I know certain skins of pale satin that may not be robust, but have nevertheless a most elegant bloom. Why should I deny myself the delight of fondling them? Can you give me one good reason? Because you love me? I am very gratified, highly flattered, but should I banish all lovely creatures because of that?"

His luck held till the very end. At the last he knew for certain that he was truly strong. It was, at bottom, the proof he had been desperately seeking all his life. Very nobly, he managed to have his head cut off during the revolution of '89. Céline, for her part, was equally convinced that this time he had made a fatal error of judgment. So each of them took the guillotine as a sort of yardstick, but they were not measuring the same thing.

Busy safeguarding her own peace of mind, keeping carefully away from the places where her husband enjoyed his conquests (except on a few rare occasions which had soon left her embarrassed), Céline had led a most discreet life. It was doubtful whether the existence of a Madame de B. was even suspected. This discretion saved her life. Moreover, her sturdy body and her way of walking made her seem a typical peasant; her bitter sufferings had reduced her to a state of utter stupefaction not unlike the misery of the average citizen; and its ravages showed clearly in her face. No government spy, no civic guard, no robber troubled to give her a second glance as she walked across Paris, bundling up her skirts to step over the streams of blood. Yet in those skirts she had sewn four pounds' weight of diamonds, and in the little bag swinging from her arm, under some hunks of mouldy bread and a bitten-off sausage, she carried her necklaces and bracelets, her ear-rings and brooches.

In the thinly populated stretches of the High Alps where Théus stood, folk were slow to understand the workings of Liberty viewed as a matter of national policy. The few men in this part of the country who took an interest in this aspect of the Revolution were well-fed horse-dealers incapable of imagining life more than a stone's-throw from an inn. They never looked beyond the estates in the valleys, the flood-plains, the dairy farms and cattle-breeding pastures. In the hamlets of mountain and forest, the poor peasants and woodcutters accepted the Rights of Man with a nobility of soul worthy of the days of old. One has to be an aristocrat in some ways to seek one's fortune above a certain altitude. They had no fault to find with the old Marquis de Théus, and they did not take advantage of the Proclamation of Universal Rights of Man to exploit their own. Céline found her father again, still leather-clad and lean, almost as much a Wandering Jew as ever, and until the year IV they listened to the sounds from the valleys together.

The first civil administration of the Directoire that was installed at Gap renewed the shipyard contracts. One night, Céline stuffed her long chemise into a pair of breeches borrowed from her gardener and climbed the thick ivy covering the north tower. In her pocket she carried a sharp pointed trowel, and with this she neatly loosened two large stones just below the parapet and far from any window or embrasure. Working with her little dagger between these stones she hollowed out a space large enough to slide her hand in, and here, one by one, she hid her diamonds and her other jewels. All too clearly, the moon showed her the depths of the precipice she was overhanging. Her thighs were large and muscular, but the ivy branches were very old. Yet she had the nerve to climb down, filch some tar and harness wax from the stables, mix it with plaster to make a sort of mortar, and then clamber back up with it to seal the stones securely in place. She was beginning to feel that she might yet make something of her life, but she was equally well aware that she would probably need money to do it.

For some time now, Pierre had appeared in her dreams not as a martyr with his head under his arm, but simply as an ordinary fellow with his head on his shoulders as in life. Sometimes she would believe he was actually with her, his presence seemed so real. That night, when she once more set foot safely on the solid ground below the tower, she dared to speak to his ghost as she had never dared speak to the living man. "Now then, Diablon! What d'you think of that?" she said quizzically, and went to bed realising that at last he belonged only to her. There she tossed and turned till daybreak before she fell asleep, beside herself with happiness.

The wheedling officials of the Directoire, the casual happy-go-lucky way they signed bearer bonds and paper money terrified Céline. So did their impressive timber contracts with as many zeros in the totals as there were pebbles in the Durance. She understood the value of a zero. Once she knew that Pierre's spirit was ready to step from the shadows into the light of day, she also knew that, though she had possessed hardly a centime's worth of the living man, she could easily have the whole of his ghost to herself, provided she could afford to surround herself with an oasis of silence, solitude and leisure in which to dream. That was when she stuffed her chemise into a pair of breeches and climbed the old ivy.

The Bankruptcy of the Two Thirds, which swept away eighty per cent of all fortunes and filled the year XII with weeping and gnashing of teeth, proved her right. Had she not taken the precaution she did, she could have been tempted to dip into her treasure to help those who were hard pressed. But she did not don her gardener's breeches again. She took to riding astride a mule and accompanying her father wherever his business took him, even into the roughest shipyards. She resolved to learn how to handle workmen, and always struck precisely the right note in those complicated affairs that involved dignity, politics and la Patrie.

It was she who renewed contracts with the Consuls, resuming for that purpose her own name and her title of "Demoiselle". On the watch for everything that could strengthen her resurrection, she noted that in this mountain canton the title of Théus had the force of a symbol, a brand that marked every tree for leagues around, whether standing or felled, a trademark that guaranteed fair dealing, backed with a prestige that had endured for many centuries. "That is real nobility," said she, and became very noble herself.

The old Marquis died quietly in his comfortable bed, a very sumptuous one for those times, and for two years the Marquise de Théus very closely studied the workings of social administration under the Consulate, taking particular interest in the assessment of taxes, the civil code, the activities of the Banque de France. She was always calling on the Prefects, questioning them, noting down their replies in her large, awkward, aristocratic handwriting, bewildering them by her careful attention to detail. They could not guess that, in everything she did, this woman of thirty was hurrying to keep a love-tryst with a phantom.

At last she went one day to the servants' quarters and said to her gardener's wife: "Marguerite, give me a pair of your husband's old trousers." Next morning she left for Gap, then for Marseilles, and was away twelve days. When she came back, she had a birdlike vivacity amazing to see, as though she were covered with kingfisher feathers and her clumsy body had wings. At once she sent Dominique into the mountains to summon the overseers and workmen; she called in all her people, lined them up in the great salon and walked endlessly to and fro before them while waiting for the latecomers, her skirts billowing with her great strides. The spritely gestures of her hands and head, the gaiety in her voice, her quips and pleasantries set them all at ease, and the last mountaineers arrived to find the room echoing with bursts of laughter. When everyone was there, she called gently for silence.

"I am an old woman," she said. There were vigorous protests, and truly she had never seemed so young. "I am old," she repeated, "no one knows it better than I, and it suits me very well. But it is not right that a hand of bright young fellows like you should be ordered about by an old woman." For more than an hour she talked to them, suddenly disclosing the extraordinarily intimate understanding of these people that she had acquired so secretly, so patiently. She spoke their own words in their own tone of voice; knew their hearts and their love of justice, equalled their blunt candour and their broad Gallic humour. Open-mouthed, they listened to themselves speaking.

She amazed them still more when she explained her purpose in telling them the facts and figures that simple folk love. She placed entirely in their hands the organisation of her estates, specifying precisely what work must be done, naming the men who would take charge, giving them all she owned in such a way that nothing was lost, a point that filled them with admiration. Then, with tears of joy streaming from her eyes, she dismissed them one by one, choking back the sobs that shook her though her broad face shone with light.

She closed the door behind them and placed her hand on her heart. Now she was free to savour, second by second, every minute still to come. She drew the curtains across the windows, and opened the wide inner doors so that the full length of the three salons could symbolise the magic avenue through which Pierre had first come to Théus. She herself lit every candle in the sconces and candelabra. Then, on the battlefield itself, she paused before the tall central mirror and, with supreme irony, gave herself a new beauty. Suddenly she had the skill and perception to leave untouched the places where tears, bitterness and age had left their mark, but lightly emphasising with a hint of blue, a touch of rouge, a little powder, those features now made lovely by her joy. She was already wearing full evening dress, so restrained in its grandeur that none of her people had noticed. Her shoulders were covered only by a shawl that was crossed over the throat he had never liked. She went to sit at the far end of the last salon, in an armchair that held her stiffly upright. There, in the exact centre of the perspective, she waited while the velvety candle flames flickered through the vast solitude reflected in the mirrors. "Well, Diablon?" she said, and he appeared at the other end of the avenue of light. He came swiftly towards her like a giant, like a ship, like the darkest day of the Passion.

But as time went on she found the phantom as disappointing as the living man had been. He had brought with him all his emotional trappings; he could do nothing else, for his egoism was of the spirit rather than of the flesh. In vain did the Marquise glorify his face and body, she was once more forced to swallow the same mortifications. She had wanted time to remember; now she had it, but she remembered everything. Cruel deceptions practised on the young bride now made the old wife pause. She had time to consider them closely, turn them this way and that, examine their motives; thus she wounded herself with sordid tricks that formerly she had passed over lightly. But Pierre's shade still remained as necessary to her life as Pierre himself had been, and she wept till she understood how futile necessities are in general. Then she took herself in hand, and the day came when the cruellest wounds seemed trifling.

She never again closed the dividing doors of the state rooms, and every evening the candles were lit (quietly, by her maids), but it is impossible to heat these vast spaces. The masts of the whole fleet of Toulon would not have been enough. She therefore had her sedan chair installed in the end salon for greater warmth. Once settled inside it with her wide skirts, her shawls and her great body she was very soon comfortably snug. Sometimes she even fell asleep there. She had learned that the wounds of self-esteem, even of love itself, are not really cruel unless one's body is frozen. That was her first lesson in the way of the world.

She had another little bout of fever during Napoleon's rise to power. By nature she was passionate, rather than aristocratic, and she admired the usurper. "Ho ho," she would say, "would you have preferred him to be beaten?" Every day the battlefields set free so many young men's souls that a spirit of youth hung like a cloud over the whole of Europe, just as the dust hangs over a field where chalk is being ground. She invented a son for herself: "He's just like his father," she would say. "Isn't he handsome! Such a rascal!" Like a child whipping a top, she speeded up his growth, and a few months later he was twenty. She arrayed him in full regimentals and sent him to join the Emperor's suite, but on the night of Austerlitz she killed him. "Those one loves," she said, "should die at the peak of their glory."

Now she was forty, she busied herself with household matters. She grew fond of food and rather selfish. She had a double chin, her jowls hung down, and she gazed at her phantom through a lorgnette. She began to go out a little and take part in society – the society of Gap. She disciplined her manner and appearance, girded up her loins, instantly raised whatever barriers she needed to protect her personal liberty and peace of mind from the world at large. She became somewhat malicious, but was honest enough not to spare herself, and on some evenings she barely had time to reach home and the refuge of her phantom's arms before collapsing into bitter tears.

She remained, however, within the bounds of good manners. The cruellest barbs never went beyond her thoughts, and in her wildest actions her high rank and the traditions of her mountain home never allowed her to go too far. Once she was sure of this, she gazed at a little portrait of her brother Laurent and murmured: "You see, you were wrong, virtuoso."

She tolerated no disorder except when she was busy with her pots and pans. There were no garden fruits, or even wild ones for ten leagues round, that she had not preserved or made into jam. She would spend all day with her skirts pinned up, her bare arms covered elbow deep with fruit juice, jellies, compotes, while she mixed, strained or decanted the results of her labours, surrounded by preserving pans, vats and cauldrons, all filled with bubbling lakes of jam.

Foreign travel was fashionable at the time, and a popular explorer had written a book on Finland, called *In the Land of the Lakes*, that was widely read in the provinces. On her good days, the Marquise would stroke a lady's cheek, (tomorrow she might ravage it with one of her salty sarcasms), and say: "You are lovely, my dear. Do come and see me at home in my own Finland of jam."

3

As the coach bounced over the cobblestones of Gap, Angelo awoke. Day was dawning. The Marquise was still asleep, her face puffed and blotchy. "What trustfulness," he mused. "These are people after my own heart. After the desire of my heart, rather," he corrected himself, "for I am much more wary. If I had been accosted out in deserted country on such a dark night by an unknown man, perhaps I might also have taken him up in my carriage, but I should have kept my hand on my dagger all the rest of the way. How delightful to conspire with people who can be so reckless!"

So concerned was Angelo not to be made to look a fool by the wily French, he had not noticed, indeed had been quite unaware of the serene moonlit night he had spent on the road. Despite the white corduroy suit he wore, he kept thinking he must look quite forbidding.

Dawn was shedding a pale green light over the shabby little houses they passed on the outskirts of the town. Though here the valley was still hemmed in by the high mountains, the first fresh light of day had reached the avenue planted with small maple trees. It was extremely wide, giving promise of a town of some importance. On the grassy rides that flanked the road, flocks of birds were stirring up little clouds of dust, their chirping plainly audible in spite of the noise of the coach on the cobbles.

They slowed to a walking pace to pass a long line of waggons loaded with great casks of wine on their way up into the Alps. The carters had tightened their blue smocks at the waist with leather belts and were walking with their hands in their pockets, bending forward and stamping their feet in their high boots.

"There's a north wind getting up," said the Marquise, who was now awake. Angelo hardly knew what to say to such a woman. She was so completely at ease, and in any case did not seem to be bothering about him. He contented himself with smiling as gallantly as he could, but to himself he said: "I must look silly. She'll take me for some stupid boot-licker, and think she has shown me a great favour by saving me a few leagues' walk." So he put on a solemn, almost lordly, expression that would have been offensive had his face not been so young. The Marquise found it most amusing.

The carriage entered a courtyard. "This is where your stagecoach starts, my lad. But wait a bit," she went on, as Angelo jumped to his feet. "This carriage will stop when I tap with my stick on the panel that Dominique is leaning against, as you see I am doing now. It is only afterwards that one gets down." Somewhat abashed, Angelo begged her pardon for his unmannerly haste, and this time his smile was truly charming.

"Where are you going?" she enquired, smiling kindly in response, touched by his sensitive features. "You remind me of a puppy trailing his long ears."

"I am going to Aix," he replied, stiffly pompous and blushing to the roots of his hair.

The Marquise glanced away, biting her lip. "That isn't any longer a matter of government concern," she observed, still smiling. "Plenty of people make that sort of journey nowadays, without it being noted officially. Take my word for it. So go and talk with that fat man over there, the one spitting on his doorstep like a kettle. Pay him for your seat, and I'm sure there'll be no problem. On condition that you travel outside: I know the inside seats are all taken. But," she added, checking her little hiccup of a laugh, "you won't mind that, will you, Christopher Columbus?"

Thereupon she stepped nimbly from her carriage and ordered Dominique to get down her luggage.

Whenever Angelo was irritated by anyone he considered to be kind or vulnerable he would stalk away from them, his long legs readily lending themselves to a swift yet dignified pace that he fancied was eloquent of his haughty displeasure.

In the courtyard that morning was a countrywoman showing an egg to the people standing round. The shell was flat on one side, and on this space were some crinkles that looked like the outline of a man's face, the same face, she said, that used to be on the old five-franc pieces, whereupon everyone agreed that it was clearly the profile of Napoleon. Another set of wrinkles on the opposite side of the egg was at once taken to represent an eagle with its wings outspread. "But my hen wouldn't do such a thing on purpose," she protested, naively. "I am a good royalist like everyone else." People were crowding forward to examine the phenomenon and making loud comments, till at last the peasant woman grew thoroughly alarmed, fearing that she, or at the very least her hen, would be thrown into prison.

Smoking one of those very strong cigarillos that are rolled in Tuscany, and are almost intoxicating, especially when smoked on an empty stomach, Angelo ventured to take the egg in his hands. The women let it go with obvious relief, and when he offered to buy it she willingly agreed, calling the crowd to witness that she was only too glad to be rid of the horrible thing. But Angelo rashly gave her ten sous, and at once he felt a quite singular tap on the shoulder. Turning his head, he found himself in the presence of a little man with an avuncular look about him in spite of his fierce moustaches, his belted overcoat, his top-hat and the cudgel forever twitching at his remarkably flexible wrist. "Ten sous, devil take it! I suppose, my young prince, in your eyes that little item is beyond price?"

"Now I really have run into trouble," said Angelo to himself. "This is what that fine lady meant when she called me a puppy tumbling over its own ears." In the background he could see the Marquise supervising her luggage being stowed over the rear springs of the stagecoach. "I can permit myself to indulge a whim of that sort," he remarked out loud in the caustic tone that used to provoke his adjutants. "No matter what the cost, subversive objects must never be left in the hands of the common people." He managed to pronounce the word with the appropriate grimace. "I imagine," he continued, "that a policeman's expense account does not allow him to handle such matters diplomatically. It is the duty of all supporters of law and order to see that any scandals are stifled *ab ovo*, if I make myself understood," he concluded with a serene imperturbability that he found even more intoxicating than the smoke of his cigarillo.

"Would this loafer be somebody important?" the little man wondered, and he stopped twirling his cudgel. He had been so taken aback by Angelo's casual, high-handed manner that he failed to notice his Piedmont accent. "I beg your pardon," said he.

"You were treating the matter very lightly yourself," Angelo went on, staring at the little man with his black eyes blazing.

"I was just going to interfere when you came," pleaded the crestfallen police officer, stroking his moustache. "That poor woman isn't a dangerous character, and if I hung back it was for a good reason. You will understand, sir, I expect. We have to go very gently in these small country towns." He fancied this stern young man might very well be a sort of secret agent sent down from the Prefect's office in Paris.

"I quite understand," Angelo replied, very much the

colonel. "Now I propose cooking and eating this egg for my breakfast, unless you have any objection?"

"None whatever," said the man, completely reassured. "With your permission I'll go with you to the kitchen, where they'll give you some boiling water. I'm on very good terms with the landlady. It's all open and above-board, he went on, giving Angelo a wink. He was quite at ease again. "It's very cold on the beat in the early morning and late at night, so she gives me a glass of brandy. You can have a taste too, sir." As they crossed over towards the inn kitchen the thought occurred to him: "As a matter of fact I had better seem to be doing my job properly," so he enquired: "Doubtless you have your identity papers, sir?"

"I have all I need," returned Angelo coldly, taking the workman's identity book out of his pocket and slapping it against his hand.

"He's top echelon," thought the man in the top hat. "It's perfectly all right, sir," he said aloud, pushing away the papers. "I have to carry out my duty, but that's enough. I can see the sort of man I'm dealing with." To himself he was thinking: "This chap's used to taking command. What a bright young spark! No good trying to fob him off with any fancy tales! Papa Guizot certainly knows how to choose his men!"

While this conversation was going on, the people who had crowded round the egg-woman had dispersed, but were still watching events out of the corners of their eyes. "What's going on?" asked the Marquise. "It's a tall young man in a white suit," they told her. "He has just bought an egg that had on it a portrait of Napoleon, an eagle and some rude words about our king, so the policeman asked to see his papers, and now he's being taken off to prison. He gave the woman 3 francs for the egg and was very insolent to the police officer, who was only doing his duty."

The Marquise had, in fact, seen Angelo take his papers from his pocket and then enter the inn with the *policier*. "Was Dominique right, after all?" she wondered. "Have we given a lift to a brigand? But I can hardly believe that when I remember how his velvety black eyes looked at me just now, and that sensitive bloom on his skin as he blushed for what, after all, were very mild faults. Our age would have to progress by leaps and bounds." The Marquise was approaching the inn door when she saw Angelo coming out again, obviously master of the situation and so thrilled by the burning excitement of the game he was playing that even his white corduroy suit had an air of splendour. She watched him go and pay his fare, and noticed that he took a handful of notes from his trouser pocket. "That proves he's neither brigand nor peasant," she decided, "for he stuffs his money in the same pocket as his pipe." Then she observed he was smoking a cigar. Though she had certain romantic fancies, the Marquise had always treated her own money with the utmost respect. Sometimes she would go so far as to press out crumpled notes with a warm iron and polish her coins with a piece of chamois leather. She felt a great reverence for money, for it had enabled her to satisfy her love in spite of Death.

"How unconcerned he is," she mused. "There's a being that nothing can daunt, yet he's scarcely twenty! Still, I did see him blush, and he was as furious as a turkey cock at my little joke just now about Christopher Columbus. How very funny he looked, marching away with great strides like a general! I wonder, can he be sharper than me?"

The horses were brought out and hitched to the coach, the postilion blew his horn, and she had to take her place inside. As she was arranging the odds and ends she carried with her, she saw Angelo briskly climbing up to his seat outside. The road out of Gap rises sharply for a long way, and the team took it steadily. On each side, clumps of oak trees, ethereal in their little new leaves, stood flexing their magnificent black muscles. A bright May sun had risen and the grass, still steaming with the heavy over-night dew, was as dazzling as water. Little fair-haired shepherd boys, hardy as mountaineers, were tending herds of goats in the undergrowth; they blew their little clay pipes as they came running down the slopes to greet the coach with a fanfare as shrill as the song of larks. There was such a gaiety about this early-morning start that the passengers waved to the children and threw them sous that they ran to pick up from the dust.

Angelo, on his high perch, saw all around him a vast amphitheatre of russet-coloured mountains. High into the gentian blue of the sky they thrust sharp pinnacles of ice, crowned by feathery plumes of powdered snow blown by the north wind. Here and there among the tortuous curves of the massive escarpment, where larch forests lay like strips of faded serge, the eye caught the acid green of little fields of rye, the gleaming black of a slate roof or the warm tones of thatch, the medley of colours in the cottage walls of some remote hamlet, the rainbow of spray above a water-fall. The cushiony clumps of trees that edged the road merged, further down the valley, into an oak forest where the turmoil seething at the mountains' roots was shrouded and hushed. The upward surge of earth and trees gave an additional excitement to form and colour; the whole landscape expressed exaltation, an intensity of feeling emphasised by the flickering silver flames of poplar trees in the wind; while the crows wheeling overhead increased the atmosphere of departure.

Just at that moment Angelo was bitterly unhappy. The smell of horses and the eight enormous rumps pulling the coach with such effortless ease had made him think of

Boiardo, the black horse he had sold at Briançon. "How could I leave you behind," he mused, "and sell you to such men as those, incapable of a generous thought, to judge by the way they took money from their purses. Obviously it was their sole treasure in life. I failed in friendship and in honour. I should have had the courage to cut your throat and give you a speedy death. But," he went on, chilled with shame at the word 'courage', "what a scurvy liar I am! Stupid, too, for what is the use of lying to myself? The truth is plain. I never gave a moment's thought to all the wonderful qualities of that friend, or his faithful devotion which, every day, added something to my joy of life. All I thought of was my own paltry safety. It's futile to try to convince myself that I spared him out of kindness. I simply sold him out of prudence, so as not to leave the body of a slaughtered horse in the woods to attract the attention of the police. And I talk of greatness!"

The incontestable grandeur of the mountain arena, the golden shimmering majesty of the day made Angelo's sense of his own mediocrity even heavier. The fact that he was sitting on a bench drawn by eight horses at a walking pace, instead of enjoying the freedom of a morning canter through fan-shaped lights and shadows, struck him as significant.

But the coach now breasted the hilltop and a flick of the long whip set the team galloping down the slope beyond. The postilion blew his horn to clear the road, and as the fanfare burst upon Angelo's ears his mood changed. "Friends have their own rights, I must not forget," he reflected after a moment. "Boiardo is free to choose how he will die. I have no right to impose on him my way of seeing things, and if my need of grandeur goes so far as to make me stab to death the friends I leave behind, it's a most disagreeable companion. Doubtless I was hasty in judging those horse-dealers. They were certainly very close with their money, but still they may perhaps be capable of appreciating the beauty of a gentle sensitive creature. You are so delightful, Boiardo, that they couldn't help loving you. You must be in some mountain stable, knee-deep in hay so fragrant that even men find it intoxicating. Or, thanks to your lovely lines, your nobility that no one could fail to notice, perhaps you have already been chosen by one of those warm-hearted women like this old Marquise, who would be such a good soul if only she would stop talking."

Angelo's neighbour was a man of fifty or so, with a thin sunburned face, muffled up in a caped overcoat of faded tartan. In his hand he carefully carried his hat, wrapped up in a check handkerchief, and on his head he wore an old deerskin cap. "My young friend," said he, "I must tell you that we can all see your lips moving, and your pensive air will deceive nobody. I watched all that happened in the inn-yard. You certainly acted very rashly down there, but it is infinitely more imprudent to reveal so openly that you are still so concerned with that affair. Believe me, there's little likelihood that the police officer will put in a report about it, he'll go no further than the warning he gave you. You looked guilty enough to make a whole posse of police jump to their feet."

"I assure you," Angelo replied, "that I was certainly not still thinking about that ridiculous incident, which, in any case, turned out very differently from what you imagine. Actually, I was reproaching myself for my conduct towards a very dear friend whom I left a day or so ago."

"I congratulate you," said the man in the overcoat. "Such scruples are rare in a man of your age. I am all the happier at the way things have turned out."

"But," Angelo went on, "I saw no harm in buying that egg."

To make themselves heard above the din of the galloping

horses they were obliged to shout, consequently the coachman and postilion sitting in front of them heard, too. When
the egg was mentioned both men turned and winked at
Angelo, laughing so uproariously that all their teeth showed,
and making a highly irreverent gesture with their hands,
obviously at the expense of the police.

"There's your answer," said the tartan-clad traveller
genially. "One can spend a hundred years trying to cure a
fever, an illusion of grandeur, and still have to beware of
relapses." He leaned over Angelo and spoke in his ear. "You
had the excuse of youth, and you are high-spirited, as anyone can see from your eyes. The same reasons could not
apply in my case, yet I was on the point of doing just
what you did, except that perhaps I should have had the
prudence to give the woman only one sou. And – who
knows? – perhaps not. Like everyone else, I was very
attracted by that magical manifestation. The common
people have every right to a measure of glory, and, make
no mistake about it, what they were all admiring with
open-mouthed astonishment was not so much the memory
of a great man – very far from what we have now – as
the mysterious workings of nature in using the egg-duct
of a hen to remind them that they were once masters of
the world."

He finished whispering in Angelo's ear and sat back, but
went on smiling, sometimes at visions of his own, sometimes with his eyes turned towards Angelo. With the hand
that was not holding his hat he gestured to indicate that a
great deal remained to be said, but the noise made by the
coach and the galloping horses, and the wind buffeting the
ear-flaps of his deerskin cap, prevented his saying it then.

The winks and the expressive by-play of the coachman
and postilion had delighted Angelo. "Here is the true heart
of the people," he thought to himself, "and the devil take

the rest. 'We'll do as we like, and all the police in the world won't stop us.'" He felt a surge of ridiculous pride when the driver turned and said to him: "Tell me, sonny, have you got in your pocket the brother of that little cigar you're smoking?" "I've got its two brothers, and even a few little cousins that aren't bad," replied Angelo, offering cigars to the coachman, his mate and the man in the overcoat. "If you find it too breezy up there," the driver went on to the pair of travellers, "come and sit down here between us. It's rather a tight squeeze, but we can all crowd in together."

So driver and postilion moved over and made room for Angelo and his fellow-passenger, who was still carrying his hat. The coachman was a huge blond rustic. The sleeves of his old jacket were cut off at the elbow, showing forearms as big as the thighs of a ten-year-old child, covered with thick red hair full of dust and oat grains. The smell of his sweat was very forceful, very masculine. His thick bright-red lips were pursed around the cigar he was smoking, so that his face seemed to be sealed with a great blob of scarlet wax. Angelo, crushed up against him, was at the peak of bliss. Under the eyes of such a man as this, to win approval from his great round mouth, he would gladly have jumped into the midst of a corps of gendarmes like a ball in a game of ninepins. "Men like him deserve to be free," he said to himself. "None of my own fellow-countrymen would have dared to say to me anything so sublime as the suggestion he made just now, that we should all crowd in together. What a natural genius for the right tactics to adopt in the fight against tyranny! Back home, even the bravest and most sincere lovers of equality and freedom always have a little grin of self-conscious reticence. Even when they know nothing of the circumstances of my birth, 'your lordship' is forever on their lips when they talk to me. Yet wasn't I the same there as I am here?" ·

He had completely forgotten the fine uniform he wore as Colonel of the King's Hussars, and the outstanding qualities he owed to being the secret son of Ezzia, the Duchess whose little cat-like face, great violet eyes and lovely robes embroidered with gardens of romance, were a nightly enchantment to anyone prone to passion. In his opinion, the countryside he was now passing was the fairest in the world, and he was deeply moved by his glimpses of a farm wall, a man on foot, a wayside shrine, a village, and the fields he saw wheeling past, covered with poppies and cornflowers.

They had reached that straight, two-league stretch of road leading to the bridge of La Saulce. "Hold tight, gentlemen," said the driver. "You shall have a taste of speed, if that's what you like." The horses lengthened their stride to a gallop, taking magnificent delight in their own swift-ness. You could watch them urging one another on, thrusting forward against the collar, and now and then, in full flight exchanging brief caresses with their muzzles.

After crossing the bridge the coach halted at La Saulce to pick up the mail. "Some folk like a good English gallop," remarked the coachman, "and some like cherry brandy. Mother Martin, that fat woman you can see over there in a blue apron idling on her doorstep, could serve you some that's well worth the journey." Angelo invited the others to join him in tasting it. The postilion accepted; his mother, he said, had advised him to drink something strong in the mornings. But the passenger in the caped coat declined. "Do you know that stuck-up fellow at all?" whispered the coachman. "No," Angelo replied. "Then keep mum," he advised. "He's right," said Angelo to himself. "I'm always far too open with everyone." He would have given any-thing to possess the coachman's scowling brows, his heavy, suspicious eyes.

The Marquise saw them go in the bar. "This boy has charm," she thought. "He's already surrounded with new friends, and I'll wager it was to please him that that fat fool, Bastien, had us all galloping along like mad things just now."

Towards noon they stopped to change horses at a long low inn with the sign of *La Part-Dieu*, standing by itself among the fields, beside a clump of evergreen oaks still decked with the streamers of a country fete. A meal was set before them on tables in the open air – tripe beautifully prepared with wine sauce. After enjoying several helpings, for this was a favourite dish of his, Angelo was strolling in the sunshine when his fellow traveller came up with him. He had now got rid of his old travelling tartan and was wearing a cape of midnight blue, with a very fine pleated cravat of white lawn that threw into startling relief his lean tanned face.

"Well, my young friend," he began. "Dreaming of your love affairs?" He was now wearing his hat tilted lightly back over one ear, and amusing himself by slapping his gloves against his thigh.

"This would not be the right moment," Angelo returned, giving him no encouragement.

"All moments are good," said the other cheerily, and was about to say something more, probably something saucy, for a glint of malice sparkled in his eyes, when the Marquise, who had opened her sunshade and seated herself on a bank, saw him through her lorgnette and called him. Angelo turned his back and walked towards the thicket of oaks.

"Where have you sprung from, you old dog?" asked the Marquise.

"Out of the same box as yourself, dear friend," replied the man in the coat, bowing to kiss her hand.

"Don't tell me you were at Gap this morning! If you were, my eyes must be playing me tricks."

"Your eyes weren't deceiving you," he assured her, "but I was wearing a tartan travelling coat and a cap."

"What!" the Marquise said. "It was you in that caped coat? I saw that, of course; from the back, I should say. But who could have imagined ... and just now, during our meal, I was eating like a countrywoman with my nose bent over my plate and did not notice you. Where are you going, then? What tricks are you up to now?"

"If I have to tell you a lie," said he, "I am on my way to Marseilles to settle a trifling dispute ... a difference of opinion on an ecclesiastic affair."

"You're as far from church matters as I am from being beautiful," laughed the Marquise.

"Ha! Ha!" he responded gallantly. "Do not force me to confess the secrets of my heart."

"As though anyone would ever succeed in making you confess to anything at all," said she. "And that charming young man, lofty as a cypress, who just now was privileged to receive your kind advice (never disinterested, as I well know), is he, may I ask, one of those churchmen whose differences you are to settle?" and she gave him a long, steady look through her lorgnette.

"Answering you frankly this time, he is exactly the opposite."

"'Frankly' is an odd word to hear from you. I don't mind telling you that just now you looked as if you were licking your chops! It was precisely that incredibly guileless look you always put on for an important occasion that attracted my attention and made me recognise you."

"I don't dispute your term 'important occasion'," replied the man in the cape. "What else can you call it when you come across a man so honest that he has no hidden motives; at least," he added with a smile, "one whose hidden motives are even more generous second time round. To tell you

44

exactly what happened, I seized the chance of revelling in his sheer youthfulness. The young man's natural simplicity enchanted me, and God knows I could do with some enchantment!"

"That's what I call a quick summing-up," commented the Marquise.

"One doesn't need to be a magician to understand him," the man went on. "He betrays himself in the first three words he speaks, and his fourth tells you all the rest. If you had not interrupted us just now, I wager he would have gone on to talk about his mother, who, incidentally, must be a remarkable woman, to judge by the seductive charm she passed on to her son. Look at him; notice the way he carries himself; such easy grace as that means one thing, valour. I need no other proof; there it is in complete perfection, with all its dash and verve. And there's a dignity about it, too, that enhances its quality, for dignity is an essential part of conscious valour. Look at his upright bearing and the way his breast swells (why? God knows! in all probability simply because, while idly dreaming, he has just noticed in that field down there some splash of colour or some flicker of light that has a noble beauty). Think of his nostrils, which I cannot see, I'm sorry to say, but which must be dilated like those of a horse when he smells hay! All that means pride, dear friend, but the finest kind of pride, which drives a man to overcome himself. As for those two or three movements of the head he's just made, I don't need to be near him to know that he is watching the foliage of those green oaks with the passionate joy most men feel, or used to feel, in my day, only when gazing on the face of the woman one loves. Believe me, if he were to die I should be grieved, but I should buy his skull for Lavater, who would find in it the fairest proofs that man can be sublime."

At that same moment, as a matter of fact, Angelo, striding

along beside the clump of trees, was saying to himself: "Who will teach me to recognise hypocrisy? Or even to acquire the plain common sense that coachman has? That man's keeping his eye on me. Could he be another Baron Schwartz? But this one has a sharp nose. It wouldn't be at all wise, this time, to let him have a sword. Anyway, I'm not going to strew my path with corpses."

"But what about you, my dear?" the man in the cape was saying. "May I ask where these bad roads are taking you?"

"Prepare for a shock," said the Marquise. "Laurent has just been married."

"What! That old wolf? A real wedding?"

"Has he ever done things by halves?" she asked.

"Alas, no," said he. "But, at his age . . ."

"He has no age," she replied.

"That's true," he agreed, suddenly very grave, "he is ageless, like that other one."

"What other?"

"The angel of the shadows, my dear friend."

The Marquise lowered her lorgnette and sighed.

The horn was blown to recall the passengers, and Angelo saw the Marquise give him a friendly little wave of her hand as she resumed her inside seat. He returned her greeting so magnificently that everyone noticed this young workman in white corduroy, who bowed in such courtly fashion.

There was a new relay at Manosque towards six o'clock in the evening. "My young friend," said the man in the caped coat, "I think your stock of cigars is running low. Have you ever tried this French cigar that they call a 'crapulos'? Although it is milder than yours, I think it will meet with your approval. Shall we step over to that tobacconist's? Between ourselves, this is the sort of cigar French workmen smoke." He still had his hat and his deerskin cap. "Don't be alarmed," he added.

"There's no need for me to answer him," Angelo said to himself. "All this is to trap me. I don't know anything about the cigar he speaks of, and I'm supposed to have lived in France for a long time."

There was to be a change of coachman and postilion at this point, as well as of horses, and the men who were being left behind came to collect their tips, holding out their hats to the company. "What's the usual amount," Angelo wondered, so he watched the other. When he put in three francs, Angelo did the same. The coachman tossed the coins up and down in his hat with obvious ill-humour.

"That rascal," thought Angelo, "was expecting a tip of ten francs from me. Now he has the insolence to show contempt because I conform to custom. He has not the slightest sympathy for my inexperience. All he saw was my rashness, and the profit he might make out of it."

4

W HILE MORALISING THUS, ANGELO had unconsciously
been watching the man in the cape and finding his activities more and more intriguing. He had just been talking
to the new coachman, obviously with considerable authority, drawing the man aside into a corner of the coachhouse
and unquestionably giving him binding instructions to
which the other paid careful heed, bending his head to
listen and now and then responding with a little nod of
comprehension and assent.

With a nonchalance that Angelo would not have found
in the least suspicious had his attention not already been
attracted by these unusual manoeuvres, the man in the cape
began turning his attention to the three passengers waiting
to join the coach at Manosque, three quiet, unassuming
men like notaries' clerks. He prowled close by, taking a very
long time to light his cigar with a lighter that seemed to be
giving him trouble, and apparently trying to catch a word
or two of conversation, but the three men were not talking. They stood watching the cobwebs on the ceiling with
an air of complete unconcern.

The man in the cape strolled over to the hand-luggage
the men had put down near the coach, ready to be loaded;
three gladstone bags, very old and worn, but carefully
mended; the sort of thing a thrifty housewife manages to
find and patch up when the head of the family has to go
on a journey that can no longer be avoided. The man
in the cape dropped his lighter between the bags and
had to move all three of them, swearing audibly, before he
managed to find his little silver box again.

"Well, my young friend, it's getting dark now," he

48

remarked when he had settled himself again in the imperial beside Angelo. The coach had just pulled out of Manosque and was moving at a trot past the great fountains and dark shadows of the road for Aix. "You're going to be cold; your clothes are very thin," he went on, as his open hands groped searchingly over Angelo's jacket round the pockets. "Did he feel my dagger?" Angelo wondered.

"You're a disconcerting fellow, my friend," said the man in the cape, his voice suddenly grave.

"I don't see how," Angelo returned. "Almost all of us have something to hide. It's only people who forget that who find us disconcerting."

"And so I am very politely put in my place, I suppose," answered the man in the cape.

"No more than you were before," said Angelo. "You remarked that the cigars I smoked were not usually fancied by a man of my position. As a matter of fact, my position is not what you may think. My clothes are obviously borrowed, and I had good reason for borrowing them. As long as you don't try to probe any further than that, you're no worse placed than I am."

"The darkness has made you bold, my lad."

"Boldness breeds boldness," Angelo retorted. "The dark makes no difference."

"What a vulgar idea," he thought to himself. "Why should he imagine that I'm bolder when it's dark? How different he is from the woman at Embrun! She used her eyes and saw how things were, as clearly as if I had killed Schwarz in front of her. I had to tell her lies to keep my secret. This man sitting beside me has nothing in his mind outside the Register of the National Debt and the tricks that can keep a man's name on the right side of the ledger. The best way to keep my secret safe from him would be to tell it to him outright. My only risk would be that he'd think me mad. But he might, on the other hand, decide I was trying to tease him, and then he'd turn cold and reserved, a most unpleasant atmosphere to have beside me, especially when life is as exhilarating as it is at this moment, galloping along through such a night, bright with moonlight and full of the scent of pines."

The night had now settled in, but the moon, newly risen over the hills, was shining upon the edge of a thick forest bordering the road, its firm outline broken here and there by pale boulders or the towering trunks of huge pine trees. Further on, the road followed the bank of the Durance, which here was very wide and cluttered with islands, each of them breasting a shining furl of water like molten lead. Then the river turned aside beneath clumps of willow, while the road ran on into a clearing where the fields shone bright with half-grown corn. The valley narrowed sharply. The coach slowed to a walking pace to cross a bridge slung between two crags. The swaying of the bridge as it sagged under the weight of the coach, the depth of the gorge with the waters churning far below; the roar that echoed between the sides of the narrow chasm, the chill breath rising from the gulf, all gave Angelo a tremendous thrill. Life was wonderfully exciting!

His thoughts ran on: "The moment I get to Aix I must find the man whose name and address those comrades gave me. Though he's from the Tyrol, to judge from his name, he must be a hot-blooded zealot, since it's in consequence of an adventure like mine that he now lives in exile. But I distrust the cool heads of mountaineers. If he's married and has a family, I shan't stay long. I shall politely take my leave and be off to enjoy freedom in my own way. With what I'm carrying in my belt I can dress like a prince and live like a lord for a year or more. The important thing is to live here as I would have lived in Piedmont, and not to lower my standards till I gradually sink to wearing a cape and nursing my hat for economy's sake. I killed the Baron to liberate my country from a foreign yoke. At least, that's what those three little terrified hypocrites solemnly assured me when they gave me the address of the man in Aix. How they quaked with fright when they realised that if I agreed to leave town I should go only in broad daylight, wearing full uniform! But for their burning lust for power, the frenzy that is always working in them from head to foot, it would have given them jaundice! They couldn't find words bitter enough to express their disapproval of the duel I fought with Schwartz. 'There was no need for such high-flown scruples.' they said. 'Idealistic nonsense!' Yet it is precisely such ideals that give me an interest in life. Otherwise I should never have found the patience to listen for hours to their abject tirades without losing my temper. All those mean little speeches on 'grandeur' and 'magnanimity' they treated me to, while in their faces I clearly read their self-interest. Mere nobodies, who would do anything in the world, no matter how base, to make themselves important! My companions in nobility, that is to say perhaps three or four true-hearted men out of all the thousands now fighting, will be their dupes in the end. Our country will throw off one yoke and bow under another. The second will be just as heavy, if not heavier; the prisons will still be full, but the men in them will be different, that's all. A farcical idea of liberty, if in the end we simply pass from one master to another!

"In reality, they were delighted at what they chose to call my stupidity in giving the Baron a sword. I watched them rubbing their hands together as they left the palace, probably saying to one another: 'Now we shall be well rid of this aristocrat who has never done anything to make anyone hate him, and who, with his romantic mother and fine clothes, would have turned out to be a dangerous rival. Even if he is arrested, he's so pig-headed that he'll never give us away. Besides, even supposing his scruples, his fine airs and graces, wear off when his shackles get a bit tight, it will always be easy to prove that the whole affair was a conceit of his own, and nothing to do with us.'"

Angelo was no longer bolstering up his enthusiasm with memories of the French Revolution, as he had done the night before. The Frenchmen he had seen were wearing shabby coats, being over-careful with their hats, feigning generosity with three-franc tips. "My 'fine airs' are precisely what I intend to keep," he said to himself. "What national liberty will ever give me more joy than my own freedom? Nothing sublime can be enjoyed in common with others."

The coach was now tearing along at full gallop under a leafy tunnel of branches dappled with moonlight, when suddenly the driver reined in his horses at a crossroads. "What are you doing?" demanded the man in the cape. "I have a passenger getting out here," answered the coachman.

As he jumped down from the box and moved towards the back of the coach to take off some luggage, the man in the cape leaned over the carriage door as it opened. "Stop!" he shouted. "Don't touch that luggage. What can you be thinking of, my dear lady?" he went on. "I give you my word there can be no question of your following your whim here. If you recognise the authority I possess, be kind enough to get back into the coach. Let us push on as far as Peyrolles, it is only a league further on; you will be able to dismount there in comfort. It will not take you much out of your way, and I will tell you something to convince you that my advice is sound."

"I need no authority or advice but my own good sense," said the Marquise calmly and forcefully. "I can stop at the place I'm going to, I imagine? Come on, lad. Hand me down my luggage."

"Listen to me, Céline."

"What do you want me to listen to? Speak plainly."

"Well I cannot call out secrets of state here on the road!"

"Oh, my friend," said the Marquise, "there's not the slightest chance that your vehement manner will make me go two leagues further than I must," and she walked off towards the coachman who was carrying her luggage to the roadside.

"Céline, come here," urged the man in the cape. "You cannot stop here alone tonight. At this particular spot, I mean."

"But I am not alone," she replied. "Laurent's coachman is coming to pick me up."

"He is not here."

"He will be, in a minute. I'm not going to rush off to Peyrolles like a fool, just because his watch happens to be slow."

"Be quick and make your mind up, sir," called the coachman, who had climbed back to his seat. "I've got my hands full, trying to hold in the horses. They can smell their stable." In spite of all he could do, the coach wheels had in fact already made a couple of turns.

"Céline, I can leave you anywhere else you like, but not at this place on this night," cried the man in the cape.

"If Madame has need of an escort . . ." said Angelo very courteously, rising from his seat, moved by the urgency in his neighbour's voice.

"Hey, sir! Mind your own business," the man retorted, and pushing aside the postilion he jumped down into the road.

"Hey, sir! That's just what I am doing," Angelo replied, as he also jumped down. The horses jostled each other and broke into a gallop.

Scarcely had Angelo reached the ground when he felt himself seized by his coat collar, while something hard was pressed against his waistcoat. A voice that he hardly recognised as that of the man in the cape said to him: "Keep your hands away from your pockets and don't move."

"You will agree, dear friend," observed the Marquise, "that some explanation at least is due to me. Are you two coming to blows over *me*?"

"First let me see to this fine young man," replied the man in the cape. "I mean to find out what his game is."

"My game is very simple," Angelo returned coldly. "Madame helped me last night. It is only right that I should help her tonight. And if you are still bothered about what's been puzzling you ever since this morning, my name is Angelo Pardi. I am a colonel in the King of Sardinia's Hussars, and I left Turin after running my sword through a certain Baron who insulted my country. I had no quarrel with him personally, but, as for you, I have found your manner towards me thoroughly objectionable all day. Furthermore I warn you that for more than a minute now I have been holding against your stomach a dagger so sharp that it cuts through lead like butter."

"The devil!" said the man, his voice perfectly steady. "This is what's called playing poker. But, young man, have you anything to prove what you say, other than your fine airs?"

The term "fine airs" reminded Angelo of his reflections ever since crossing the bridge, and thoroughly restored his good humour. Ignoring the hard object still pressed against his waistcoat, which could only be the muzzle of a pistol, he openly put the dagger back in his jacket pocket and took out his ring from his fob.

"Perhaps the moon is bright enough to let you read what is on this seal, if you have good eyes," said he gaily, and in spite of the pistol still levelled at his heart he recklessly stuffed his hands into his pockets.

"My friend," commented the Marquise, "I rather think your ace has been trumped. Your expression is most amusing."

"You're just a child, Céline," returned the other, "and, God forgive me, so am I, to let people talk before I kill them. Take back your seal, sir. I trust you, but you must obey me instantly. I give you my word there isn't a second to lose. Help me carry this luggage under cover."

They took shelter under the dense shadow of a holm oak whose branches swept the ground. Barely a moment later they heard a galloping horse. The side road joining the highway lay in bright moonlight, leading down from the black rolling hills beyond to cross a little level clearing in full view of the oak.

"That's not your brother's coachman? At least, I hope not," the man in the cape whispered to the Marquise.

"I don't think so, either," she replied, "unless he means me to ride pillion."

The horseman rode into the clearing. "That's no yokel," said Angelo. "He rides so superbly that his horse is revelling in it." There was, indeed, something unusually high-spirited and harmonious in the horse's rhythmical gallop, like a skilled gambler playing a winning sequence in a game of chance. The rider pulled up at some distance from the crossroads and approached the highway at a walking pace, taking care to keep his mount on the grass verge to make no sound. At the crossing he halted, and grew so still that he seemed under some magic spell. Not once did the horse champ his bit; his long tail hung as straight and stiff as though it were of iron. The horseman wore a tight riding coat girded at the waist with a belt, and the glint of his buckle never flickered. Though he had not sought to conceal himself in the shelter of the trees, he was so well placed at the fringe of the wood, where the moon was shining through the leaves in a patchwork of light and shadow, that he became invisible.

The night was full of the song of nightingales answering each other under a sky as resonant as the vaulted roof of a church. "He's lost in a dream," breathed the Marquise. The man in the cape put a finger across his lips. This fascinating stillness lasted for some time, but at length the rider began to move with the utmost caution, coming nearer to the oak and even brushing its branches as he passed. His face was completely black. Under his felt hat he wore a mask of dark material that hung down over the collar of his coat. He crossed the main road, making less noise than the nightingales, and moved under cover on the far side.

"Unless I'm much mistaken," the Marquise whispered, "that was one of the celebrated churchmen you were talking about this morning."

"And you can congratulate yourself," replied the man in the cape, "on having made me miss a very pretty little secret conclave." Turning to Angelo, he asked: "Are your eyes sharp?"

"They're excellent, sir."

"Then look to the left of that tall poplar down there, just beyond the cornfield. Don't you see some little dull gleams?"

"I can see them perfectly," Angelo replied, "and if you want my opinion I should say that three or four horses are down there, not as well managed as the one we've just seen. They're shaking their curb-chains." A moment later, the watchers could make out certain glimmers that suggested the horsemen were on the move. In fact they soon left the shelter of the thicket and came forward one by one into the moonlight. They crossed the field at a walking pace, in

Indian file, six of them in all. A hundred yards from the oak they waited in a group under the poplars bordering the high road, until from somewhere in the copse spreading from that point to the bank of the Durance there came a signal like the hoot of an owl. Then, one after the other, like birds hopping, they jumped a ditch and vanished among the trees.

"Have you any idea what it all means?" asked the Marquise.

"Yes," replied the man.

Angelo had very sharp hearing, and was as keenly alert as if he were on the warpath, fighting Austrians. He turned his head, and saw, through the thickly hanging branches of the oak, a horseman standing motionless only ten yards away. Taking infinite precautions to avoid the slightest rustle from the bed of dry leaves where he lay, he pointed the man out to his companions, urging absolute silence. This sentinel was a man of very different calibre. Though, like the others, he wore a mask, his head was bare and the moonlight threw his elegance into strong relief. At length he seemed to reach a decision, and moving down the bank as silently as a snake he crossed the road and vanished like the others into the woods beside the Durance.

"That's the one," said the man in the cape, "who, like me, knows just what's going on."

"How irritating you are!" said the Marquise. "Don't imagine that all this impresses me in the very slightest, or will make me forgive you for that ridiculous scene just now. I could perfectly well have watched all these goings-on by myself."

"None of your spoilt child airs, if you please, Céline," answered the other, "and be good enough to speak low. Besides I fancy your coachman's coming. I can hear wheels on the road from Peyrolles, and I don't think the Marseilles coach is due for half an hour yet. It's bound to be him. He must have been more sensible than you, and have gone to wait for you at Peyrolles. I must ask you to do me a service," he went on, addressing Angelo. "Take charge of this lady. I have the weakness, and so have all her friends, to love her naughtiness and her complete lack of common sense. Stay with her and accompany her wherever she goes. Do not leave her until she is safe and sound at her brother's door. I give you my word that tonight it is a task that any soldier would regard as an honour. You told me you are a colonel. Treat her as a colonel should. If you succeed in getting her away from here as she is now, I shall have the greatest respect for the military training schools of the King of Sardinia. Do not bother about me, either of you, and do not mention me to a soul. Take the luggage and go down to the roadside. You have seen nothing. If anyone questions you, play dumb. You may well be questioned very cunningly, so be on your guard. I am sorry I cannot offer you one of my two pistols, but I shall need them both. Still, you showed me just how well you can rise to an emergency."

"It's so funny to hear you talking with this comical air of assurance that I am amply repaid for all your impertinences, dear friend," the Marquise replied. "As for this brave lad . . ."

"Come, Madame," said Angelo, and taking her by the hand he led her out from the shelter of the tree.

The coachman had pulled up at the crossroads and was looking in every direction, cracking his whip. "Call out to him yourself, Madame," Angelo advised her. "He is not expecting a man, and my voice might alarm him." The coachman seemed terrified already, and did not pay the slightest attention to Angelo. "Get in quickly," he said roughly and hustled them into the carriage, threw the luggage into the boot, jumped up to his seat again and whipped up the horses so fiercely that they backed in disorder. Then they plunged forward at a gallop along the side road whence the first night-rider had come.

The vehicle was a sort of farm-break mounted straight on to rigid axles, and the jolting was terrible. Every moment, the Marquise and Angelo were thrown against each other or against the leather sides, which fortunately were well padded. At last, after perhaps half an hour of this risky speed over such rough roads, Angelo grew so furious at this insolent buffeting that he managed to kneel on the front seat and pull aside the leather curtains. Seizing the driver by the collar he shouted to him to stop, in a voice that the horses obeyed even more quickly than the man.

"Unless you do as I tell you I'll slit you up like a dog," he cried. "I'm not accustomed to put up with any nonsense," and he went on wildly at random about soldiers, the hussars, even his duel. Mention of the duel seemed to make the coachman pull himself together. "I thought I was doing the right thing," he said, "to get along as fast as I could and avoid the fogs of the Durance. They are bad, and can give a man a fever he won't get over."

The carriage had halted at the crest of a hill where the wind in the pines sounded like the waves of the sea. Suddenly Angelo, who during night watches at camp had often heard haphazard firing by nervous sentinels, caught the sound of two or three faraway reports that he recognised as pistol shots. At once he remembered the advice of the man in the cape. "You did well," he said coldly. "There's nothing more dangerous than those fogs you speak of. I know people who have died of them. However, now that we are far enough away, drive with a little more caution otherwise Madame and I are likely to knock each other out. We could die from that, too, and I tell you flatly we should never forgive you. Our ghosts would come and drag you around by your feet every night. Are we likely to run into any more of your celebrated fogs on our road?"

"I don't think so," answered the coachman, "but the best thing is to get on and not dawdle too much." He added that in any case the hill track they were then following, which here and there sloped dangerously down towards rocky ravines that yawned white in the moonlight, would soon bring them to a much better carriage road.

"Very well," said Angelo. "Madame and I prefer to risk the fog until we get to that road, so, till then, drive at a walking pace, and open up the leather curtains on each side so that we can enjoy the countryside. It's very beautiful tonight."

So far the Marquise had said nothing, thoroughly enjoying Angelo's prudence while, sly as a cat, he talked of the fog. Now she asked the coachman why he had not waited for her at the crossroads. He was just about to climb back to his seat, but he came to the window again and, without answering her question, demanded roughly whether there was any need for explanation on that point.

"You're such a fool," said Angelo sharply, "that your own stupidity is the best explanation, I suppose. It's lucky for you that we so much enjoyed listening to the nightingales in that wonderfully peaceful spot, otherwise you would already have heard more about it from me than your ears could take in." Reaching through the window, he seized the man by his thick woollen scarf and shook him so violently that he overbalanced and had to clutch the mudguard to stop himself from falling. "Learn to do as you're told, and don't try to act on your own initiative again," Angelo ordered him. "Speak politely, listen carefully to my commands, and you may still have a chance of dying peacefully in your bed."

"I beg your pardon, sir," answered the coachman, pulling himself together, "but I didn't know who you were. I assure you I acted for the best. I hope you'll forgive my very natural ill-temper, for it was a very tricky situation when I found that Madame had dismounted at the crossroads. Please remember, too, that I did arrive in time." Angelo scarcely listened to what he was saying, and dismissed him with a peremptory wave of his hand.

They went on down the hill at a walk. The view was magnificent. The full moon, riding high in a cloudless sky, was so bright that they could clearly see the whole landscape, even the distant vineyards clinging to the hilly slopes on the far side of the narrow plain that lay as flat as a sandy shore below them. A chain of very rugged little black mountains barred the horizon with fretted cliffs, fringed by the tossing branches of arbutus and terebinth. Forests of pine trees, pale as foam, billowed as far as the eye could see. But the night, merging all colours into one, made everything look unreal, and Angelo began to watch the scene with wonder and awe, as a man gazes at a hero.

"We must talk very quietly," said Angelo. "This rascal is now certainly trying to catch everything we say. I don't know who he takes me for, but since I will not tolerate any rudeness from him, and I should be particularly sorry to have to thrash him in your presence, I think it is best to leave him in error. Have we far to go?"

"We have to cross that little plain down there," the Marquise replied, "make our way into a gorge on the far side, and follow it to the top, where there is a sort of plateau, called La Vallette. It must be three leagues further."

"I am amazed," Angelo went on, "that a boor like this should have been sent to meet you. He has no idea how to pay you proper respect."

"I'm not easily surprised, myself," returned the Marquise,

"but I must confess that everything amazes me tonight, and not least the fact that I am in your safekeeping."

"In spite of the advice of the man we left under the oak," said Angelo, "if you wish me to leave you, I'll go at once."

"And what will you do here, where you do not know the country?"

"Sleep under a tree and wait for daylight."

"In that case," she replied, "you might just as well sleep at the inn at La Vallette."

"Am I a child?" Angelo thought, wonderingly. "This coachman I grabbed just now knows how solid my fist is, and he's ready to call me "my lord" any minute. But this woman, whom I cannot shake, except with words, treats me like a little boy. I don't know how to make her appreciate me properly. It's only in action that I can show my worth. People who know how to talk can readily foster the good opinion, or at least the just regard, of those around them. Then they can sit quietly on their benches or in their arm-chairs while their reputation grows by itself. But I, I have to act. Shall I still have time for living?"

He indulged in a few very Italian reflections about the Marquise, watching her out of the corner of his eye. He despised her inability to appreciate anything out of the ordinary. "I much prefer those imaginative women," he mused, "who exaggerate the sensational side of things, and imagine that any townsman in the streets after midnight must be a villain swathed in a dark grey cloak. What a thrill it is to walk beside them in the dark! How they tremble and squeal and cling to my arms! They make me fully aware that they are women, and I am a man. If there is nothing to fear, they invent something! That's youth! This woman has never known what it is to be young.

"At heart, she has no conception of the joys of life. Rarely have I been as happy as I was just now, lying flat on my stomach in that bed of dried leaves with masked men all around us. The slightest movement of my hands and legs became vitally important. I love the chill that comes over me and makes my perceptions so acute when danger is near. But she is so thick-skinned. Such people can never know the difference between heaven and hell. Their own little hells and heavens are so commonplace that they pass from one to the other without noticing any change. I'll wager she would find a host of silly reasons for poking fun at me, if she knew that under my shirt I'm wearing a scapular dipped in the blood of St Januarius. How different she is from my mother, who can read signs and portents even in the bright noonday sun!"

He had no very clear idea of the significance of that group of horsemen, and imagined that perhaps they were performing some rustic rites or other round the holm oak where he and his companions happened to be sheltering. "But . . ." he said sharply, speaking aloud.

"But what?" asked the Marquise. "You are wriggling about on your seat like an insect on a pin. As a colonel, perhaps you have second sight that has warned you of an ambush? Or are you not quite easy in your mind about the gentle walking pace at which my coachman, by your orders, is driving us through these charming woods? I expect your squadron carries out some very funny manoeuvres when you are in command! You have attached too much importance to the words and actions of my honourable friend. I know him well enough to be quite aware that the wisest course is never to be disturbed at anything he says or does. We are in France, my lad. As for that Red Indian phantasmagoria he made us watch just now, any sensible person will dismiss it for what it is worth. Doubtless some young farmers on their way to an open-air ball, who met to pass the word on to their friends."

"You are probably right," replied Angelo, taking pains to choose phrases that were punctiliously courteous, if over-long. "But is it any fault of mine if, though I have known you only since last night, it gives me pleasure to think I am affording you some protection? I agree, the nights in France seem extraordinarily peaceful. You do not need me, and can send me away whenever you wish. However, since you were kind enough to allow me to glimpse the possibility of finding a bed at La Vallette, you would be doing me a service if you would keep me with you until we get there. But I've just been reflecting," he went on to himself, less cere-moniously, "that you know more about it all than the rest of us. Why did you insist on leaving the stagecoach at that particular crossroads? Your brother's coachman would not have lost his head and been so rude to you for anything as unimportant as a simple country ball. Frankly he acted like a man in a blue funk. And then, he asked you point blank if there was really any need for him to explain why he was so terrified. As for the sentinel I spotted last, stationed ten yards behind the oak where we were hidden, he looked no more like a farmer than I do. I can judge the cut of clothes pretty well. Besides, his horse was a beauty. The man we saw first in the moonlight rode another just as fine. Real thoroughbreds."

Their driver parted the leather curtains and called, "Here we are at the main road, sir. Can I gallop a little while, now? It would be a great help, for it would be best for us to be home before eleven." "Ask Madame," Angelo replied.

All the time they were galloping across the narrow plain Angelo was thinking delightedly of the way he had said "Madame", and how successfully he had managed to con-ceal, behind gallant phrases, his own shrewd perceptions of what was afoot. Once or twice he thought about the man in the cape, with a good deal of pleasure. "He's enjoying himself, but so am I. He needn't have advised me to be cautious. Such people will never fool me."

"What a charming creature he is!" mused the Marquise. "His heart is as sensitive as the bloom on his cheek. I can do what I like with him. All this is most entertaining, quite apart from the fact that if he were not here I should be terrified. I don't in the least understand what is going on."

5

"Is she really a marquise?" Angelo wondered. "When my mother comes across an intrigue like this, she handles things very differently. What couldn't she have made of masked cavaliers and moonlight! Instead of being so churlish and matter-of-fact, she would have been honey personified! She'd have used the devil's own wiles to charm any man audacious enough to volunteer to protect her, as I did for this so-called Marquise! True, my mother is a duchess . . . and moreover, a duchess of the House of Sardinia."

But when they reached La Vallette he saw the chateau dominating the village. It stood on an eminence crowned by tall trees, their lordly branches swaying to reveal, in the bright moonlight, the pale façade of a very lovely house, in style pure French eighteenth century. Narrow flights of steps, such as one finds in Siena, led up to it directly from the road, and on the crest of the hill stretched balustraded terraces whence rows of lights shone out through the blackness of the park. Angelo had to admit that it looked truly noble.

The coachman knocked with the handle of his whip on an iron sign representing the sun, and in spite of the late hour the innkeeper was most polite on recognising Madame. "So she's a real Marquise after all," said Angelo to himself. "Why does her spirit lack the harmony of that beautiful house commanding the whole countryside? Why has she none of the appealing grace of those trees that have needed the tender care of five generations to reach such magnificence?"

He listened to the liquid sound of a light wind in the

leaves of huge beeches, while the night-capped landlord, not daring to interrupt his reverie, stood waiting, candlestick in hand.

The room to which Angelo was conducted with much ceremony was vast and surprisingly elegant. A magnificent counterpane, embroidered with a profusion of silk flowers, covered the bed. The pillow case had floating frills of lace, and the turned-back sheet was of damask. A very fine armchair in glowing red corded silk, trimmed with green, stood like a throne beside a table on which were set a leather writing case and an inkstand with new metal pens.

Angelo, who had not slept in a bed since leaving Turin, was ready to drop with weariness. Hearing a knock at his door, he called: "What is it?" "Your wine, sir," answered the landlord, bringing in a little silver carafe and a glass on a tray. "This is what's lacking at the inns of my own unhappy country," Angelo reflected. "This natural urbanity that, without one superfluous word, brings you on a tray a sense of being at home."

He slept so soundly that he heard nothing of a very loud storm that broke out towards five o'clock in the morning. When he awoke, the rain still fell in great showers and the thunder was growling in the distance, while the densest black clouds were piling up again. Angelo decided to wait for a settled break in the weather before enquiring about a means of travelling on to Aix. Perhaps he might even be able to hire a horse at this inn. He felt fresh and in good heart, and the prospect of continuing his journey alone on horseback appealed to him enormously.

Still the storm raged on. The single street running beside the park was deserted and the rain made a great noise in the trees. The public room of the inn was gloomy, and Angelo paced to and fro a hundred times or more between the huge fireplace and the window before he noticed in a corner an object that attracted his attention. It was a gladstone bag. He easily recognised it as one of those he had seen loaded on to the stagecoach at Manosque, the previous evening.

The house was very quiet, except for a steady rustling sound like the noise made by a file of sharpshooters marching through ripe hay, and loud enough to be clearly heard above the drumming of the rain on the beech leaves. Angelo pushed open a door. It gave on to an immense stable with a vaulted roof, where a large number of horses – Angelo counted eighteen of them – were hungrily feeding from the racks, standing motionless except for the movements of their heads and jaws, as exhausted horses do. They had not been rubbed down, and the saddle marks stood out darkly against their sweat-covered hides. The light filtering through the window slots was dim, but Angelo could see that some of the animals were very fine.

Towards noon, the rain, instead of clearing, settled into a heavy downpour. Though Angelo had given no order, a meal was beautifully set out on a table in the embrasure of the window, with an indication that it was for him. He wondered where the party of horsemen might be, and with a gesture towards the stable he asked: "Where are the others?" "They never stay here," replied the landlord. "They have gone on up. Their horses will go up tonight." He ate heartily of jugged boar-meat, very well prepared, and was served with a silver carafe of wine, the same vintage that the landlord had brought to him the night before, but then he had been too tired to appreciate fully how good it was. "She is certainly a marquise," said he to himself, "and all this must be on her instructions." He had slept without noticing the quality of the sheets and blankets, but he remembered the quilted counterpane, the lace on the pillowcase, and the wine glowing like a garnet in his glass.

"All this," he mused, "has the same noble air as the long façade, so pale, so aristocratic, that looked out at me through the branches when I arrived last night. If there were a woman with the beauty of that façade I should fall madly in love with her."

He was lighting his cigar when a man entered. He recognised the coachman he had handled so roughly the night before, as the man came up to the table, gave a military salute and held out a letter. "From the chateau, Colonel," he said.

"And how do you know I am a colonel?" asked Angelo.

"I ought to have guessed it when you got into my carriage," the man replied, "but I was so worried about you know what. Otherwise I couldn't have failed to realise who you were, from what people say." Though he was still standing at attention with his fingers at the seams of his trousers, he smiled with easy-going frankness. For a peasant he had wonderfully white teeth. "That's very sharp of you," returned Angelo, slowly and diplomatically.

The note was a formal invitation, expressing in flowery terms the hope that *Monsieur le Colonel* would call at his convenience. "So that detail gave them something to think about," Angelo said to himself. "My mother knew what she was about when she used her influence to get me into a uniform with gold on the sleeves. The habit still makes the monk. But since this velveteen suit I'm wearing has no gold braid, and the note mentions my convenience, I shall make it convenient to go on quietly smoking my cigar."

"Very good," he said aloud, with the correct degree of hauteur to mark his rank. As the man turned to go Angelo added: "Wait. Stay here out of the rain. There's no point in getting drenched. You will not be in my way." He forced himself to yawn very widely without putting his hand over his mouth. "That always gives sergeants a very good impression," he said to himself. "I must keep this man here till he fully understands that what he brought was an invitation, not an order."

After waiting a good quarter of an hour, feeling all the time like a cat on hot bricks, Angelo at last threw away a reasonable butt of unsmoked cigar and went over to the door, flexing his legs as though to relieve some stiffness in them. "And now, let us obey," said he, still in a tone of casual friendliness. He saw that it was still raining hard and added: "These civilians mean us to get thoroughly soaked."

"My orders were to go back and bring down the carriage at whatever time you said," the man replied, very politely, "but since you told me to wait . . ."

Angelo bitterly regretted that he had not thought of the carriage first. "That's what I should have done," he reflected, "but she thought of it before I did. Oh well, if she thinks she can tell me what to do, I'll show her!"

"Anyway," the man continued. "I can dash up those two hundred steps four at a time, and if *Mon Colonel* will wait ten minutes . . ."

"Spare your legs," Angelo replied. "I do not have a carriage on the battlefield, and it rains there sometimes too. I'll shelter under your umbrella and we will go up your celebrated flight of steps together." While the man was protesting that the Colonel must have the whole of the enormous blue umbrella, Angelo was sharply reproaching himself for what he had just said. "And what war have you ever fought in, to be so proud about it? Do you imagine this Frenchman knows nothing of history? It is useless for you to try to learn prudence. Your first impulse is always a bad one! Unless you stop and think for a quarter of an hour before saying a word, you'll make yourself a laughing stock, or get yourself hanged. Perhaps even both . . ." In the end he forced the man to share the umbrella by taking his arm, and they set off together through the rain towards the steps.

The man, who bore himself like a soldier, was so careful in a quiet, unobstrusive way, to avoid jostling Angelo as he walked close beside him, that Angelo ventured to glance at him. In his eyes he read warm appreciation, and said to himself: "Provided this fellow doesn't think too much about history, I have made a friend of him."

The flight of steps, built of very white, rough-hewn stones, made a turn and passed under the trees. The rain had brought out such a scent from the foliage and the earth, the grey sky was so soft, the sounds from the drenched parklands were so forlorn in the solitude, that Angelo's thoughts turned again to the beautiful pale façade awaiting him higher up, and to the irresistible fascination that a woman's face would have for him, if it possessed the same harmonious loveliness. "If such a woman exists, I am lost," he said to himself, trembling with the thrill of that thought.

As soon as he reached the lawn that formed a sort of ceremonial forecourt, he ran forward to the chateau. "Would *M. le Colonel* be so good as to speak in my defence?" asked the man. "I shall surely be reprimanded for having allowed him to climb the steps with me." "Go off to whatever you have to do next, and don't be afraid," replied Angelo. "I never desert my friends." This declaration of friendship left the man standing dumb with amazement. Angelo leapt up the three broad treads of marble leading to the terrace bordered with orange trees in tubs, and opened for himself the magnificent diamond-paned door at the main entrance. "Announce Colonel Angelo Pardi," said he to the footman in the hall.

The servant hastily vanished into a corridor. Angelo remained for a moment alone with the silence of the house. At last he heard brisk footsteps approaching, accompanied, however, by the sound of a walking stick, and the Marquis of Théus appeared. He was tall and lean without being emaciated, and his bearing displayed uncommon vigour. Angelo had time to note the wizardry of his tailor, who, without exaggerating the shoulders of his long frock-coat, had used all his art to reveal their breadth. A deep scar drew the corner of his right eye down to his cheek.

"Colonel," he said, smiling, "you have terrified my footman. Your sudden appearance made him believe some god or other had arrived. He babbled so incoherently about it that I came to see for myself. Do excuse him. He is not accustomed to seeing a Saint George break into our Thebaid. Come, my dear fellow, we have been waiting for you." He took Angelo familiarly by the arm. "Ho, ho! This is an arm to justify all François' terrors! Do you know," he went on, while they both walked the length of a corridor, its windows darkened by climbing roses heavy with rain, "that you rescued my sister from a fine hornets' nest? Are you aware of what happened?" But Angelo was aware of nothing except a very subtle fragrance of incense that perfumed the corridor. "Then," the Marquis continued, "listen while I tell you. My sister herself does not know everything. Last night the Marseilles diligence was held up, not four paces from the crossroads where you were so foolish as to wait for my coachman. That my sister knows. A strong box belonging to the General Treasury was stolen, and three of the plainclothes police who tried to guard it were shot dead. That is what my sister does not know. Don't think about the three dead men, look pleasant, and come in to receive the thanks we owe you."

Before being thanked by the Marquise, who rose from her seat and came forward as nimbly as her vast haunches permitted, Angelo was introduced to a guest. He had never seen a French bishop before. This was one. Accustomed to the dapper Church dignitaries in his own country beyond the Alps, Angelo was astonished that this man had the clumsy heaviness of a peasant. His hands, in particular, were those of a ploughman, and on them the episcopal ring looked out of keeping, like some stolen jewel. He had cheeks like a cornet-player. "He's bursting with health, but his eyes look jaundiced. He's only an *in partibus*, not a local diocesan," Angelo was thinking to himself when he heard himself curtly addressed.

"You were, it seems, present when this affair was going on last night."

"Only the preliminaries, my lord," Angelo replied.

"It would be advisable for me to know exactly what you saw," said the Bishop.

"In my opinion, very little," commented the Marquis, "and that confirms the account Céline has given us."

"Your opinion is beside the point, my dear fellow," the churchman returned, rudely enough. "I want the precise facts."

"You won't get them unless you stop waving your hands about," the Marquis replied, his voice icy.

"I beg your pardon," said the Bishop in a conciliatory tone, while his face fell naturally into an expression of great benignity.

"Now at last he does look like a bishop," Angelo thought to himself. "When I came in, he was probably scared at the idea that he might run into some danger on the highroad one of these days. That's what gave him the jowls of a bulldog just now."

"You have taken the wind out of my sails," said the Marquise, "and now I don't know what to say. I had it all worked out so well, too. Are you still a colonel, my boy?"

"There's no reason why I should stop being one," Angelo answered in some surprise.

73

"Well, we never know where we are with a man like you," returned the Marquise. "I like surprises that follow one upon the other, but yours only go off once, like a firework. Last night you announced that you were a colonel, in such a startling fashion that I fully expected some prodigious promotion, and that by today you'd be Alexander or the Archduke himself. How disappointed I am!"

"That's not the sort of question to put, Céline," the Marquis observed. "Miracles will not come for the asking. As for me, the moment I set eyes on him just now I compared him to Saint George, simply from seeing how he routed François, who was on guard in the hall. If you must have something to surprise you, feel his arm. It's like iron."

"I don't think much of surprises that have to be touched," the Marquise retorted.

"My dear," said the Bishop, "let us hear what the young man has to tell us. I assure you, he'll be more of a surprise than Alexander to the Marquis and myself, if he proves to have played merely the part of Argus."

"French seminaries must be veritable hotbeds of alchemy," Angelo thought to himself. "Now, this peasant's face looks as profound as though he were a real scholar. Madame la Marquise has undoubtedly told you," he went on aloud, "that we were hidden under a holm oak."

"I know the place very well indeed," said the Marquis. "Which tree did you hide under?"

"I have never actually fought in a war," said Angelo, "but I have very often been on manoeuvres close to the frontiers of our bitterest enemies. I set my whole heart on learning how to sum up in the twinkling of an eye the terrain where I might have to fight one day. So I can tell you very precisely that we were under the round oak that stands five paces from the highway and overlooks the side road leading in this direction." His little preamble, quickly spoken, was to punish himself for the lie he told the coachman about his war service. The Marquis remained lost in thought, his chin sunk on his cravat.

"Are you surprised?" asked the Bishop.

"Yes, I am," replied the Marquis. "And at that moment," he went on, "Bousson was with you?"

"Who is Bousson?"

"My sister has told us that one of her friends was with you, and took charge of the situation."

"If you mean the man wearing a cape, he was with us, of course, and I must say he seemed to know exactly what was going on." This made the Marquis drop his chin on his cravat again.

"I fancy," he said at last, "he has always been a little in love with you, Céline, hasn't he?"

"And have you any idea what it means to be in love with anyone or anything, a man like you?" the Marquise replied. "I have known Bousson forty years. He is kind and always ready to help me, but that's all there is to it."

"It shows exactly the sort of love I was speaking of, Céline, when a man is kind and helpful for forty years. What does Bousson do?"

"What do you mean, 'do'?"

"Has he a job of any sort?"

"You know very well he has not. He is passionately interested in anything he can't explain, and that other people can't explain either. He spends all his energies in trying to solve such mysteries, coming and going in great leaps and bounds. Then, one fine day, he decides that particular problem is settled, and starts running after a fresh shadow that no one else can see."

"In any case he has no official position, to your knowledge?"

"What a difference from the man he was when he came

to greet me in the hall just now," Angelo said to himself. "See how he's drawing in his horns. I should think more of a man whose eyes blazed with reckless daring. He is terrified to think that someone might come and smash his windows one stormy night! Tonight, perhaps! Is it merely that he's particularly fond of those delightful little diamond panes giving so much character to the great glazed door I pushed open a short time ago? Or is he trembling for fear someone will rob him of a treasure chest that he knows he's too weak to safeguard? Yet when I first saw him I would have wagered he was a man after my own heart. But where is it coming from, this fragrance one breathes in this house? Does the Marquise use perfume in her leisure moments? I have never smelt anything so entrancing." And once more he was in love with love.

"I shouldn't know anything about that," said the Marquise. "How could I? What sort of official post do you fancy he might have?"

"In the police," replied the Marquis.

"As a matter of fact," the Marquise began.

"As a matter of fact what?" asked the Bishop as she paused.

"It is fortunate for you, my lord," retorted the Marquise, "that I was well brought up. Religiously, I mean. It has always kept my temerity within bounds, and made me chary of judging church dignitaries too harshly."

Just at the same moment Angelo, on the contrary, was beginning to amend favourably his first impression of the Bishop. He no longer saw him as a peasant. He had noticed the very extraordinary keenness of his glance, and was even more struck by the fact that his face seemed hewn out of stone, his features were so set.

"I, too," said Angelo, "had an idea that this man belonged to the police. He questioned me very cleverly, and tried to corner me on matters that, in any case, I had no need to explain to him. True, for some days now I have been in a rather delicate position myself, and at the moment I am apt to see police everywhere. But I noticed his clothes, and, really, a man who dresses with such good taste could hardly belong to such an unsavoury profession." He explained at great length everything the man in the cape had said and done, putting forward several psychological reasons to prove that, in his view, his fellow-traveller was simply an inquisitive civilian suffering from boredom, a man whose spirit was rather too big for his body, who had adroitly taken advantage of every opportunity for indulging his romantic fancies. He was fortunate enough to give a brilliant account of his conclusions, and he saw that he had particularly interested the Bishop.

"My young friend," the churchman interrupted him, "if I may so address you despite the high rank you have so rapidly gained – I congratulate you with all my heart. This truly is observation. I can see M. Bousson as clearly as though he were standing before me. Indeed, even better, as if he were made of glass." He felt obliged to preach a little sermon on how clearly the soul can be seen through the body, like a light through a lamp-glass. Completing the cycle of his theme, he likened Angelo to a man who cleaned lamp-glasses, which was not at all to the young man's taste. "No wonder you are merely an *in partibus*," Angelo thought to himself. "There is nothing noble in your imagination. You collect your similes from the kitchen, instead of finding them during a hunting gallop. If you could do that, you might be able to break through the clouds on your horizon and get into a real bishopric with a palace of solid stone. I certainly hoped you would spare me that sort of old-fashioned unctuousness. You were lucky enough to spring from the people. Why did you not retain their vigorous freshness? That would have been a master-stroke."

But as the Bishop stopped speaking he licked his lips, as sacred orators do, since their voice must carry clearly under vaulted roofs, and Angelo saw the red tip of his little tongue. Immediately, as though a mechanical gear had slipped into place, his face took on an air of deep cunning, while his glance, sharp as a needle, slid through his half-closed eyelids. "The devil!" Angelo said to himself. "This man has more than one trick up his sleeve! But, in my country, bishops come from bishops' families; this little man from beyond the mountains, in spite of his breviary, will not get the better of me."

"And," said the Marquis dryly, "this lamp-glass of yours had two pistols?"

"A fellow who imagines himself a Knight of the Round Table always carries two pistols," replied Angelo shrewdly.

"A very pertinent remark," commented the Marquis.

"It didn't require much effort on my part," Angelo continued. "I often play the same game myself."

He had spoken with extreme candour, and was surprised to note that the Bishop seemed stupefied, while the jaw of the Marquis dropped in amazement. Their faces grew so serious that he went on to explain: "I am not exactly a puppy tumbling over its own ears," said he with a glance towards the Marquise. "I am well aware of my own faults. But fortunately I find a certain nobility about them. That is why I hardly bother to hide or correct them. I am a serious-minded creature. Sometimes I am taken in, because it is my nature to pay serious attention, quite gratuitously, to all the adventures that life offers me. I can well under-stand that other people, on the contrary, may consider them frivolous," and he went on to tell them, very simply, of his duel with Baron Schwartz.

The room where they sat was vast, and the rain made it so dark that they could scarcely see the walls. The windows opened on to trees, green billows rolling on to infinity. While telling his story, Angelo had more than once gripped the arm-rests of his chair, and as he passed his hand over his face he realised his fingers had become perfumed with the same fragrance that he found so lovely. "Whoever wears that perfume has been sitting in this very chair," he thought, and his voice grew so tender that the Baron's death sounded almost pleasant.

He was so placed that he could clearly see the faces of the Bishop and the Marquis. They were both extremely grave. The Marquis in particular had clenched his lips so tightly that his mouth had disappeared. At first, he cast furtive, yet very precise, glances around him, and then, still playing a part, he interested himself for a long time in something apparently going on some distance away in the park. Finally, he asked a strange question: "I imagine that you feel quite at ease with us?" (The Bishop made a quick movement, then slowly gave a lovely peaceful smile.) "Since you happened to be under the round oak, did you recognise anyone last night?"

"How could I recognise anyone, when there's no one I know?" asked Angelo.

"I attach a great deal of importance to your army rank," the Marquis went on. "You are a good horseman yourself, and you must know how to recognise the mounts of your men. If you were to meet one of those night-riders in broad daylight, would you recognise him? Perhaps by his bearing?"

"As for the two who passed close by us, the first, who was in the lead, put his horse into a trance. If he were to do that again in front of me, I should certainly recognise him. The second was the sentinel who stood ten paces behind us. I should know his figure again, and the cut of his clothes, even if he were on foot."

"What age was he?"

"Not more than thirty."

The mouth of the Marquis relaxed, and he gave a quick smile. "You are a very valuable man," he said. "Are you comfortable at the inn?"

Angelo did not stint his praises. He spoke of the embroidered counterpane, the lace-frilled pillowcases, the silk-corded armchair, and especially of the celebrated wine served to him in a silver carafe.

"Now this," said the Marquis, "was the oddest of your adventures. All those things were intended for a guest of quality whom I am expecting, and who, for certain unimportant reasons, cannot stay at the chateau. Please do not apologise. I am delighted that you have thus been my guest since last night. Besides, it is useless for you to think of leaving while it is raining as hard as this. Forget about the inn, and allow me to put at your service, for tonight, a little summerhouse standing a hundred yards away from here, in a clump of beech trees. If tomorrow the rain has stopped, as I think it will, I will lend you one of my own horses, and you will be able to ride into Aix with all the elegance you could wish."

After the little ceremony of protest on Angelo's part and warm insistence from the Marquis, Angelo gladly accepted. He was made to stay for dinner, too, and as they rose from the table the Marquis said to him: "Since you are going to Aix, will you do me a small service? Are you a chess-player?"

"That's a question you might have saved yourself," said the Marquise. "I thought you had more perception. Do you take this lad for a calculating schemer? And even if he were, do you imagine it would be with bits of carved bone?"

"That's true," replied the Marquis. "This game appeals only to men of ice-cold ambition, and you, by all accounts, are a fire-eater. I will explain the position to you in a couple of words. I hate asking my friends to do anything for me unless they understand the reason. They have the right to know what they are involved in. This is a matter that will not commit you in the slightest. Come and see. Set out on this chessboard is a game I am playing, at a distance, with the Vicar-General. No one could be more coldly ambitious than a Vicar-General, and, as for me, I am a positive iceberg of ambition. That is obvious to the naked eye. The finest thing about this game is that opponents do not necessarily have to meet each other. It's a diabolically clever copy of life. It is quite sufficient if my adversary, or, more correctly, my partner (for ambition at its ultimate point becomes as pure as geometry, and an adversary as such no longer exists) carefully keeps beside him a board like this, with the same disposition of the pieces. The squares are marked vertically with the numbers 1 to 8, and horizontally with the letters A to H, so that every space on the board has its own sign. Here is the king, here the queen; here are bishops, 'fools', as French chess-players call them (you see nothing is forgotten), here the knights and here the castles. The pawns are foot-soldiers. When I make a move, I write a note of the initial of the piece I am playing, and sign of the square it is to leave, and where it is to go. The post takes upon itself the responsibility of conveying this information to my partner, who uses the same method of sending me his reply in due course. And that, Colonel, is what ambitious men of my age play at in the nineteenth century. The game you see here has been going on for quite a long time already. If you were with our jargon I would even tell you that my queen is in serious danger. But I always seem to do very well with my knights. You see this black knight on F 5? I will move him to E 7, and so my queen is saved."

"Think carefully," said the Bishop. "You have already used your knights a good deal. Wouldn't it be better to sacrifice the 'fool'?"

"When a piece is touched it must be played, my lord," said the Marquis. "I always keep to the rules, even when I am alone. That's what makes me so dangerous."

"What wouldn't I do to save the queen," said Angelo with a laugh. "Yes, I will willingly take your little note to the Vicar-General."

By lantern light, the summerhouse to which he was escorted looked as if it had been dropped ready-made on a lawn as green as spinach. The turf came right up to the base of the walls. The place consisted of a single large room with a very high ceiling, not, strictly speaking, a bedroom, though a couch stood in one corner. For this occasion it had been spread with shining white sheets, lightly starched, and Angelo recognised the same damask as he had used at the inn. He was impressed to notice that someone had taken care to slip the pillow into a lace-frilled case, exactly like the one intended for the "guest of quality".

For the rest, the vast room seemed to be a place meant for meditation. The lovely fragrance was more distinct here than it had been at the chateau, and charmed him into a reverie, just as he was standing in front of a low bookcase where he had noticed some small volumes of Ariosto, Shakespeare and Calderón. "What ravishing creature," he wondered, "thought of wearing this perfume? I have found her traces every step of the way here, from the moment I pushed open the glazed door in that pale façade, with all its harmony and nobility. If this caustic-tongued Marquise – who has hardly spoken today, though she never stopped looking at me as if I amused her – were forty years younger, I would say it was she. In her youth she must have been well able to fly a banner of this sort to betoken her longing for perfection. But whoever is wearing this must be scarcely twenty. It is not worn to create an aura of elegance, it is Ophelia's rosemary."

The night was filled with the croaking of frogs. The trees tossed uneasily, and Angelo heard the sound of water lapping. A window looking out from the back of the summerhouse, he opened it a chink, and a ray or two of moonlight, piercing through the clouds, showed him the rush-fringed waters of a pool.

He could hardly tear his eyes away from this medallion of shining pewter, set in the dense black shadows of the park, but at last he closed the window and fell a prey to bitter reflections. "I have been wasting my life," he thought to himself. "Till now it has seemed to me a grand thing to fight to establish freedom. All I shall manage to do is to establish a set of hypocrites in every department of my country's government. There can be no nobler purpose in life than the pursuit of happiness. Even in that, too, it is hard to stay pure in heart without being fooled, but what a triumph if one succeeds! It calls for just as much courage. I let myself be misled by the illusion that quantity was of more importance than quality. The good opinion people had of me, I was willing to justify it by sacrificing myself for the good of the greatest number. But what happiness if, on the contrary, I could place my whole heart at the service of quality! Quality enshrined in the person of one woman!"

While his thoughts ran gravely on in this very childish fashion, making him really troubled, he had taken a step or two towards a little writing desk, and the perfume that had affected him so deeply suddenly made him aware of its presence in that place. "Here, beyond question," said he to himself, "that sensitive, tender-hearted woman often sits. This is where she comes to live a secret part of her life, known to no one save herself alone, and this fragrance reveals how rich it is. When she is here, by herself, she thinks her most daring thoughts, and grows as lovely as the scent she wears. No," he went on, caught up to a peak of emotion, "she must always be as lovely as this perfume, since she dares to wear it everywhere she goes in this house, and, I do not doubt, in the world at large." He did not even question how such intensely spiritual qualities could accord with the free functioning of a physical body. If the woman herself had come in at that moment, he would not have recognised her.

On the writing desk was a little porcelain vase whence the aroma seemed to come. Angelo looked closer and discovered a little handkerchief pushed into its narrow neck. He drew it out, and the moment he held it in his hand he fully understood how a man might find nothing absurd in laying down his life for such a kerchief. Then he was so filled with joy that, weary as he was, a great peace suddenly came over him and almost made him fall asleep standing up. He undressed and, still holding the handkerchief, he no sooner laid his head on the pillow than he fell into a dreamless sleep.

The birds woke him, and the wind of morning in the trees. The day was fresh and full of sunshine. At the door of the chateau a servant was waiting to take him to the stable yard. "I have had this horse prepared for you," said the Marquis. "He is a fine animal, and will not only carry you to Aix, but will give you great pleasure all along the road. Amuse yourself by making him dream, and you will see. I do not advise you to follow the road you came by, which would force you to go through Peyrolles. All the mounted police will be out, and in your corduroy suit you would be likely to attract attention, mounted on a horse that no labourer would be skilled enough to ride. I should be happy to lend you a riding coat, but I fancy you would object. Go through Saint-Paul and Vauvenargues. And here is the little slip of paper on which I noted my move at chess, which I showed you last night. On the back I have written for you the address of the Vicar-General. You can leave the horse with him, too. He will soon have an opportunity of sending it back to me. *Bon voyage*, and I thank Providence for having set me in your path. My sister feels more friendliness towards you than she has ever shown before to anyone."

Angelo, who had the little kerchief in his fob pocket, was beside himself with happiness, and would have listened with equal pleasure, no matter what the Marquis had said. He was a delightful surprise to the horse, and it could not even wait to be outside the stable yard before showing its pleasure in being free in the broad sunshine, with a rider who so well understood it.

6

IT WAS A CORDIAL INTERVIEW that Angelo had with the Vicar-General, who lived in a shady, green and peaceful road where fountains sang around his house. He was barely forty, and in the prime of an active, exhilarating life, to judge from the dimples of amusement round his mouth. He was celebrated for the sermons he enjoyed preaching to attentive congregations every Wednesday evening at Saint Augustine's.

Unquestionably, he came from a very good family. Everything about him was gracious and expansive. He walked with great strides, careless of his robes that billowed round him in truly martial fashion. Angelo found him busy preparing one of those little gems of oratory that caused a certain embarrassment, every week, to husbands and lovers, but so enchanted the ladies that many of them had phrases of his embroidered on their parasols, even on cushions.

"So this is what the old wolf has decided," said he. "If he were here, I would tell him he has mastered me. The move he has just made has spiked my guns. I have lost this game. We will start another." He spoke with the utmost good humour, and sent for some wine that was brought in by a serving maid, prettily dressed and well below canonical age. He filled himself a little pipe of amber and meerschaum. "How he reminds me of home," said Angelo to himself. "A man of quality is always at ease, wherever he may be."

He even recommended Angelo to try a certain tailor who, it seemed, could combine a Paris cut with a sound conception of English comfort. "He is extraordinarily clever," said the Vicar-General, "at giving a quiet English elegance to everything he makes, even a cassock. He is the only man you can possibly have to make your clothes, if you wish, as I see you do, to be able to mix freely in any company without attracting the slightest notice, present, yet invisible." "How penetrating he is," Angelo reflected. "That describes me exactly." Nevertheless he talked very freely to the Vicar-General about himself and his history.

He was, on the other hand, very disappointed in the celebrated "comrade" whose address he had been given. The man, an engineer from the Tyrol, had quickly found work in his own line, and was now in charge of the construction of a canal to carry the waters of the Durance to Marseilles. Angelo found him in a little plank-built hut on the excavation site, where he lived with his wife and two children in a couple of tiny rooms with newspaper covering the floor. A steam crane was hoisting its buckets, churning up a cloud of dust and hissing away but two steps off.

This man, his face half-smothered in a very fine black beard, carefully closed his door, threw his arms around Angelo, called his family together, and in their presence solemnly saluted him as a hero. With fervid zeal he begged for news of 'the cause'. His wife was feeding her baby, her hand covering her heavy breast and the nurseling's face, but at the same time she shared her husband's eagerness so keenly that her lips moved silently to repeat every word he spoke. Angelo could give only a poor response. "Come and join us," said the man. "I can give a job to everyone who has been driven away from our country. Already there are quite a lot of us, we trust one another completely and have banded together to form a lodge that could be very active." He had grandiose schemes. Angelo asked for time to think over his offer.

"I know," the man went on, "the arm that has rid us of that dog Schwartz was not made for pushing a wheelbarrow, but I could make you foreman, and we could sit together in the assembly I shall soon be convening in the grottoes of Mont Sainte-Victoire, over towards Trets." He had already built up a secret organisation that produced false documents, extremely cleverly forged, and Angelo hastened to take advantage of it.

Three days later, towards eleven o'clock at night, as he was taking a short stroll and smoking a cigar before going to bed, he was bumped into by a navvy who muttered a few inebriated words in Piedmontese and slipped into his hand a stiff-covered official passport. In it he was named as Edmond Vassard, and his occupation as "fencing master". "That," laughed Angelo, "is a joke I owe to my bearded friend from the Tyrol. He cannot contain his delight at the sword-thrust I gave the Baron, and is determined all Europe shall know of it. He is certainly an improvement on those petrified hypocrites who made me leave Turin, but I will not be a foreman."

The tailor recommended to him by the Vicar-General sent him the coat of his dreams, an impeccable riding coat of military cut. He thoroughly enjoyed walking along the boulevards of the little town, wearing fresh linen and a suit that made him magnificently "invisible yet present", in the Vicar's subtle phrase. He passed completely unnoticed among Bugeaud's young officers convalescing at Aix, crowding the cafés and the pit of a tiny theatre where, once a week, Anna Clèves came from Marseilles to sing the operas of Rossini and Mozart. Now and again, however, young girls would turn to look at him as he passed by.

Before appearing openly in the town, he had taken a few nice precautions. The day after his new clothes were delivered he packed them very carefully and walked out of the hotel, *The Maltese Cross*, where he had been staying while a little black down grew on his lips and cheeks.

He arrived in Marseilles at nightfall, just in time to get his beard shaved and his curly hair trimmed. Then he took his stand near the Hotel Versailles, and when the stagecoach from Avignon arrived at about eleven o'clock he mingled with the passengers and engaged a room. He hardly slept at all, and rose at four, dressed himself in his new linen and fine clothes, made a fresh parcel of his corduroy suit, watched for a moment when the morning waiter came on duty, paid for his room, and strolled with his parcel round the coach that was being prepared to leave for Nice. He wandered outside the inn-yard as though taking the air, and slipped into the maze of little alleys near the Aix gate, where he left his parcel in a corner.

He went on down towards the docks, where he found a café open and settled himself in the back room to write a letter to his mother. He told her, in particular, of the night he had spent in the summerhouse, and wrote more than twenty lines of romantic phrases, each more impassioned than the last, all disconnected and separated by commas. Then he went on to the quay in search of a sailing boat from Genoa, and found one in the canal of Fort Saint-Jean. Very much at his ease, he strolled up to a sailor who was smoking his pipe beside the gangway, and found that luck was with him. The moment names were mentioned, the man jumped to his feet and said to him in the Florentine dialect: "Speak low, and in pure Italian, till we can get to that breakwater over there. It is very high and quite empty. Here, take this coral necklace I have in my hand, and pretend to be trying to sell it to me."

The sea-wall he pointed out was more than a hundred and fifty feet high, and the street at its foot was quite deserted at this hour of the morning. They took shelter behind a little bastion, out of sight of the boat. "There's a lot of gossip about you back home," said the sailor, in Piedmontese, "and some people will have us believe that you're a louse because you deserted from your regiment. But no one believes that, except those it suits. Ask me anything you like, and I swear by the Madonna I will do it."

"It's a matter of taking this letter to my mother," said Angelo, "a simple thing to do, but you must on no account let yourself be intercepted, either by the porter or by any of the servants, for there must be some paid spies among them, ever since the start of this affair."

"Where does the Duchess sleep?" asked the sailor. "I will throw some gravel at her windows, and if the wall is no higher than this breakwater I can easily climb up barefoot to the bars of her room and take her the letter."

This was the first time, since he came to France, that a man had talked to him in the language of his own heart. Angelo almost crushed the sailor in his arms. "You understand me and I love you for it," he exclaimed, "but there is no need for you to break your neck. Go and idle at the corner of Pardi Square, under the mulberry tree near the fountain. You might amuse yourself washing your beret in the bowl. Watch the little door that opens just opposite. Towards four o'clock in the afternoon you will see a woman come out. She holds herself very upright and is very dark; she has a large bust and always wears green skirts. You cannot make a mistake, for she is the only woman allowed to use that door, and she treasures that prerogative like the apple of her eye. She is Thérèse, my old nurse. Mention my name, tell her you want to see my mother, and she will take you to her, up a little staircase where you will never meet a soul."

"In the first fortnight of October," said the sailor, "I shall be back here again, either on this boat or another, for it is the season for transporting wine."

"It may happen," said Angelo "that you'll be given some money for me. I rely upon you, body and soul."

"Come with me," answered the sailor, "as far as that little street over there. We will drink a glass of Asti at the house of a woman who is practically my wife. She would sooner be killed than disobey me. That is where I will leave anything I bring for you."

The woman, whose name was Paula, was enormous and walked like a duck, but her face, between her two black braids of smooth hair, was lovelier than the countenance of a Greek goddess. Her great eyes held the same sad loneliness as the wide oceans. "Beware of thin women, *mon Colonel*," said the sailor. "Absence gnaws at them to a degree you would never believe. If you go to sea for a week there's nothing left of them. Not even enough to get you a morning cup of coffee."

Angelo walked back with the seaman till they were only a hundred yards from the boat. "When do you leave?" he asked.

"In two hours."

"Then goodbye. You carry my life in your hands." Quickly Angelo turned away and took a side turning that led him to the top of the sea-wall. "Is he going to betray me?" he wondered, and from his high observation post, hidden behind an embrasure, he watched the deck for fully two hours. Then the gangway was drawn in, the little craft was towed out by a tug to the harbour mouth, shook out a sail or two and began to tack slowly towards the open sea.

Angelo went to lunch. "What will he think of me?" he reproached himself. "I did not even have the courtesy to talk to him about my love affairs. The fact is that I have none, but he would not have believed that, even if I told him so. He would have thought me proud and secretive.

I should have invented some. Yes, I certainly ought to have been polite enough to do that."

These reflections brought to his mind something he meant to have done at Aix, but it would perhaps be even easier to see about it in Marseilles. He enquired for a leather craftsman's shop, and found one in the middle of the Rue d'Aubagne, in a tiny square dominated by a bust of Homer. He wanted a little sachet made in supple leather. He was shown skins from Russia and Cordova, lovely green ones from Persia, but he insisted on a leather with no smell of its own. At last he found what he wanted and had the sachet made immediately. He asked to go through to the back of the shop and there, in front of the little glass the apprentices used when they combed their hair before going out, he unfastened his cravat. He placed the perfumed handkerchief inside the leather sachet and hung it round his neck, so that it lay against his skin beside the scapular of Saint Januarius. Then he hired a carriage and went back to Aix.

A few days later he called on the Vicar-General. "I am delighted to see you again," that friendly man exclaimed, "and in my heart I was expecting you. You are as splendid as a god, or, rather, as God Himself. Turn around! Yes, it's perfect. He even remembered to put a little silk arrow-head to emphasise all those fine pleats at your back."

"I came to ask a service of you," said Angelo.

"I could hug you for having done so," replied the Vicar-General. "I am your friend."

"I am staying," said Angelo, "at the hotel called *The Black Mule*, but dining at the communal table obliges me to join in conversations that I find very boring, and the servants who see to my room are too inquisitive for my liking. Couldn't you recommend to me a woman of respectable age who has an apartment to let, preferably overlooking a garden? If she could do a little cooking for me, and look after my linen, that would be grand. But if not, I can engage a valet." "You will not need a valet," replied the Vicar-General; "and you are making my dearest wishes come true. I even prayed to the Sacred Heart for something like this to happen. I have exactly the right woman in mind, the apartment and gardens too. I was expecting you last week, and loved you the moment I saw you. How could the Marquis let a man like you get away from him? You have seen Rosette, I think? The young woman who served your wine last time you came, and is now bringing you some more? We will drink a toast to our better acquaintance and then I will take you to her mother's house. You cannot possibly go anywhere else, not for all the gold in the world. You will really be in clover."

The Vicar-General kept up the conversation until night had fallen. Then he exclaimed: "Let us hurry there now. We have been forgetting ourselves in the delights of our new-found friendship. But that's not a thing to regret. All you have just told me about your mother and yourself pleases me beyond anything you can imagine. I have told you three times already, and I simply must say it again: I love you. Take my arm." The streets were very dark and narrow.

Madame Hortense, dressed in grey half-mourning, had something gay and brisk about her, like a guinea-hen. A great gold cross lay heavily upon her opulent, firmly supported bosom. Her ways were so precise, so authoritative in their rectitude, that it was clear not even God could escape her vigilance. She would not overlook the least slip. Now and again, though, her mouth gave her away. During the warm summer weather, when Mme Hortense was about to enjoy her afternoon nap, her lips would soften and part like an opening flower. It cost her a great effort of will to compress them again, until they looked as prim and proper as before.

She devoted herself to looking after Angelo magnificently. The house was immense, fresh and green with shade. On the first floor, two large, high-ceilinged rooms gave on to a little garden of lilac and jasmine, separated by a brick wall from the gardens of the Archbishop's residence, where great sycamores stood. Mme Hortense attended to his linen, folded his shirts, ironed his cravats, polished his floors, and watched Angelo live. "Some flowers, sir," she said one morning, bringing in three beautiful roses in a vase that she placed on a little round table. A few days later, working by degrees, she had garnished the outside of his windows with scarlet geraniums in boxes. "A lovely piece of material, sir," she observed one afternoon, showing him a length of silk from Kashmir, yellow with black spots that changed colour under the light and became tiny Persian violets. The silk hung from her fingers in folds as smooth as water, and she left it on the back of an armchair. Angelo, who was feeling rather bored, looked at it again and said to himself: "It really is lovely. It would make a magnificent cravat for the low-cut waistcoat I wear with my grey jacket." He put on his boots to go out to a café, and Mme Hortense was waiting down below to brush his coat as he passed. "If Monsieur would wear a low-cut waistcoat," she said, "he really should have that silk made into a cravat. It would set off the colour of his skin and eyes."

"How bored I am!" he mused. "My heart has been stolen by that lovely fragrance I learned to know in the home of the Marquis. In the world that perfume symbolises, life would be worth living. But not here. We must take care not to grow passionately fond of anything that is not worth the trouble."

He often went to see the Vicar-General. "Come when-ever you feel inclined," said that kindly man, "and I hope that will be every day." Another time he observed: "Basically, I am the one who has benefited most from the death of Baron Schwartz. Thanks to that, I enjoy the company of a being who is fine and brave, admired by everyone. This is where he comes to sit and pass his time congenially, feeling at home."

"The fact is," said Angelo to himself, "I should tell him everything, if I had anything to tell. But," he continued aloud, "the pleasure I take in your company (and always shall, for I feel that you understand me completely) is no compliment to you, I am afraid. No one else takes any interest in me."

"Get that idea out of your mind," said the Vicar-General, and for a moment he watched Angelo in silence. "There's nothing I can say," he went on. "Besides, you have your own eyes to see with, a mouth that can speak, and legs for walking. It is not for me to command all that artillery. God forbid that I should even wish to turn your thoughts in that direction. But, though you may think differently, you do attract a good deal of attention. Take," he continued hastily, to cut short the flow of questions that Angelo, in his boredom, was going to ask, "take Rosette herself. I have noticed that whenever you call she quickly goes and puts a little black velvet ribbon round her neck."

Rosette, who brought in their wine and tobacco, was indeed wearing round her neck a narrow black velvet band that heightened the milky pallor of her cheeks, white as lilies somewhat overblown. She did not lower her eyes, and Angelo found her glances softly languorous. When she had gone, "I assure you," he said in considerable embarrassment, "that never should I have thought. . ."

"And what would be the harm?" asked the Vicar-General. "The girl is of an age to know exactly what she is doing, and what she wants to do. Did I tell you that Mme

Hortense used to live in Mexico? That is where Rosette was born. Her father was a Spanish colonist. God, who is everywhere, as you know, is in the tropics as well as here. But there, in His infinite wisdom, He becomes tropical in spirit."

When he was home again, Angelo slipped into the garden. He was savouring the perfume of jasmine along a covered walk when Mme Hortense came towards him her eyes lowered. "A door, sir," she said, half lifting a curtain of fresh vine tendrils and uncovering a doorway through the wall. "It leads into a corridor in the porter's lodge of the Bishop's residence, and goes on into the Rue Caisserie through an alley that is always open, always deserted. If you were ever to go out that way, there would be nothing to prevent my saying you were at home, should anyone make enquiries about your movements. And if you were to receive anyone through this door, I could swear without any danger to my soul that you were at home alone. This is a most convenient house, and has always been lived in by people of quality."

"She is almost as pretty as her daughter," thought Angelo, "and though she looks so sanctimonious she cannot always control her lips. If it were merely a matter of overcoming my scruples, this excellent Vicar and this rather ripe zealot would, between them, have succeeded perfectly. But it is something much more than that," and his thoughts turned to the sublime.

"I must do something," he said to himself, "to lend colour to my profession as specified on my passport." He asked Mme Hortense for the name of a popular fencing school. "There is only one that you could possibly go to," she replied, "the Prytaneum at Cengle. It is a little way outside the town in the woods, and gentlemen ride there on horseback. The man who keeps it is a Monsieur Brisse, a nobleman from Brittany, it seems. At all events he is so elegant, so assured in manner, that he is the only *maître d'armes* recognised as suitable to teach ladies of the best society. Some of them occasionally go and watch the bouts."

"There is no need for you to buy a horse," said the Vicar to Angelo, on hearing of his intention to go and try a passage at arms with the Breton nobleman. "Am I not your friend? I'll take you into my confidence, too, and let you share the secret of my heart." He lifted his cassock, and below it he was wearing riding breeches, very well cut. "It is my pet sin," he declared, "and, moreover, one that is approved by the Scriptures. In *The Golden Legend* there are more horsemen than one can count, and then there is *The Quest of the Holy Grail*. In that courtly romance it was the Knights Templars whom the Monks of Citeaux called to bring in the blood of Christ. But in any case I go riding only at night-time, and no one will recognise the chestnut horse you'll be proud to ride."

The horse had been reared in the Bishop's stables. Angelo judged him swift, feeling his oats a little, but sound of heart. He handled him accordingly, and attracted a great deal of attention as he rode into the woods at Cengle, where a few pleasure-gardens for picnic parties stood near the fencing school. The young officers of Bugeaud's army used to spend their afternoons in these woods.

As Angelo's muscles came into play, his longing for singleness of heart grew satisfied. He put something glorious into the suppleness of his wrist and elbow, and felt his boredom drop away. "There's nothing else I can teach you," M. Brisse said to him one day when Angelo had insisted on a bout with him. "When you first came here, you still had a few Italianisms in your arm and leg movements, but now you are as cold and restrained as a Scottish

97

laird, without losing any of your own special style. Besides, what help can a school be to a man like you? You would have lost the habit of making those unproductive sweeps of your arm without any lessons from me. What else is there for me to say?"

"It was to you I came, not to the school," replied Angelo, "and don't imagine I was not speaking seriously just now. You have helped me get rid of a fault that was ruining my style, and shown me how to gain a second for every two spent in action. So, you see, your school has been most useful. I assure you I do not come here for fun, or to drink wine at the tables of those little country cafés among the trees facing your door, that to my mind are filthy and full of bad smells. I mean to go on fighting at least two bouts every day, and I should like you to criticise them minutely each time."

Then M. Brisse drew Angelo into a corner. "Tell me what is behind all this," he asked in a low voice. It was some time before Angelo understood what he meant: the man believed he was rigorously training himself in order to execute vengeance on an enemy. "There's no question of that," Angelo assured him. "I am a serious-minded man, that's all. You will never get me to spend my afternoons lolling about in arbours, or stamping on the floor like a cockerel, striking sparks from my spurs to give the ladies a thrill. I come here to give myself some purpose in life. I must have a noble occupation, and the noblest one I know is to perfect myself in the use of arms, for only so can I remain master of my honour." (For ten minutes or more he spoke very seriously on this subject.)

"If that's the way it is," said M. Brisse, "there are plenty more things I can teach you. I do not let the whole world see everything I know," and he went on to explain points that fired Angelo's enthusiasm. "I shall drive you hard. Every day I will fight two bouts with you, and each time I shall push you to the limit. Do your very utmost to resist my attacks. Reserve for such moments as that all those adroit arm movements that come to you so naturally and make you the most talented man I have ever known."

M. Brisse quickly realised the advantages he could gain from these exceptional lessons. He invested them with a certain ceremony, fully justified by Angelo's fervour, for in his fencing the young man freed his spirit from all the boredom of the little town. Though most of the school's clients were officers of Bugeaud's army, the average level of their fencing was very mediocre. Those gentlemen came there merely to work the stiffness from their legs, or to provide a plausible pretext for all the gallant rendezvous arranged in the summerhouses or even in the dense thickets of the nearby pine woods. A stiff bout with cavalry sabres was the last thing these young men wanted, their desires in this respect being fully satisfied by their past experiences or their equally pathetic future. "What is that firebrand trying to do?" they would say to one another. "He can certainly manage his sword amazingly well. But if this tall young man really wants to cut a dash, he should come with us and hunt out Abd-el-Kader."

From then onwards, Angelo lived only for his two daily bouts. He dreamed of them at night, devoted his time to eliminating any physical habits likely to cause an error, and no longer felt in the least bored. He would gaze with deep self-satisfaction at the little sachet containing the perfumed handkerchief. After a while, M. Brisse, in spite of himself, grew equally enthusiastic, stimulated by the prodigious skill he had to face, and these fencing bouts developed into exhibitions of swordsmanship that became the talk of the town. Angelo would arrive at Prytaneum towards four o'clock in the afternoon. From three o'clock onward, most of the officers and their ladies would leave the little arbours and come to find themselves a good seat around the staging. In his padded fencing jacket and his wire headguard, Angelo retained an air of great distinction. His amazing length of leg and lean muscular arms gave a most impressive reach to his sword thrusts. M. Brisse often had to jump frantically aside, then backwards like a whipped monkey. Every contest left him panting for breath and bathed in sweat.

Having taken off his padded cuirass, Angelo would again put on his short military tunic of fine cloth, the one he had had specially cut for these occasions, and gallop off, bareheaded, into the pine woods that spread a blue-green haze over the hillsides a couple of leagues away. There he would wander wherever chance led him, through the soft, clean undergrowth where his horse's hooves made no sound. Sometimes he would bathe in a little brook. All the ladies thought it a pity he was so shy.

One night, in a street near his lodgings, he was again accosted by the drunkard who spoke Piedmontese. "Come aside a step or two with me, into the shadows," said the man, his voice low and calm. They went into a covered passage that led to some granaries. "We know everything you do," he went on in a whisper. "Undoubtedly you have some splendid plan that you will not tell a soul, and you are right, though any secret would be safe enough with us I have come to let you know that, no matter what happens, you can count on us."

"What point would there be in undeceiving them?" thought Angelo. "Especially since, if there were any need for me to use my sword in their service again, I should do so. But they must let me live in my own way. Decisive moves in a revolution are never made by the men who spend their lives thinking about it. Such deeds demand an altruism they no longer possess; self-interest has tempered their ardour. As for me, I have no interest at all." But he warmly thanked the man, who, before leaving him, devotedly traced with his thumb the sign of the cross on Angelo's heart.

"You should be happy enough," the Vicar-General said to him. "You are not going to tell me now that you are unaware of the interest everyone is taking in you?"

"I do, it is true, see a great many people," Angelo replied, "and have spoken a couple of words among what passes for society in Aix, if that is what you mean, but I have no friends. Indeed, your friendship satisfies me completely. Provided you will always let me come and bother you, disturbing your studious seclusion, I consider myself the most fortunate of men." He expressed his warm affection for the Vicar in a neat little speech, and crossed his legs as though he felt quite exhausted.

"Come, now," said the Vicar, taking off his spectacles. "Tell me what it is that doesn't please you."

"I have not yet come across anyone who seemed sincere and open," Angelo replied, "and no one has said a word to me, other than the simplest conventional politeness. I have, on the other hand, read a great deal of jealousy in people's eyes, and I do not need to be an expert student of human nature to know that their lips are ready to tell the most frightful lies about me. But I swear that none of that disturbs me in the least, and as long as you like me for . . ."

"Come over here with me," said the Vicar-General. He rose to his feet, took Angelo by the hand, and led him in front of his wardrobe mirror. "Look at yourself, and tell me what you see."

"I wonder what you are leading up to," returned Angelo, who was magnificently dressed.

"To this," replied the Vicar. "First, you must listen to

a few phrases that your modesty will find distasteful," and he spoke to him in terms that such a virile man found almost unbearable, about his face and the grace of his body. "There it is, before your eyes," said he. "Forget that the man in the mirror is yourself, and judge him objectively. You are one of the handsomest men living. Your heart is just as noble, and gives you a radiance that is difficult to withstand. Furthermore, you are so totally devoid of pride that you display all these rare qualities with supreme unconcern, a casualness that, to ordinary men, implies a good deal of contempt for their own condition. But – do I need to tell you? – all the ladies find you intensely fascinating. All the gallants you meet have their own mistresses, and you have none. They all feel you are a danger to them, and have made common cause against a potential rival. Take a mistress yourself. You will make her former lover your mortal enemy, but all the other men will be reassured and come over to your side." "It is very difficult to live to suit oneself," sighed Angelo, with the utmost seriousness.

Without attaching any more importance to what he had seen in the mirror, he pondered over what the Vicar had said. "He is right," he reflected. "They are irritated because I am not like them. I must be more cunning, and seem much more ordinary. A commonplace appearance, though, will have to suffice. Further than that I will not go." He went over to see that the door of his room was properly shut, blew out the candles, and came across to one of his windows. Then he ventured to undo the little leather sachet containing the handkerchief, and savour its lovely fragrance once again. "How simple, how sublime it would be if you were here," he said. "But perhaps the woman I am dreaming of does not even exist. It is equally possible that she is ugly enough to be frightening. But this perfume, to me, is eloquent of the only kind of life I really want to live."

There were always seven or eight ladies around the open space to watch Angelo's fencing bouts. On some days even more. He carefully scrutinised them through the bars of his headguard. "Ugliness might even be preferable," he thought, "provided she was, at least, out of the ordinary. Among those women there is nothing that would interest me for five minutes, and then what should I do? I lack the hypocrisy to feign an interest I do not feel. Bah! They see no further than the ends of their noses, and it might be easier than I think. But if I am expected to adopt the stupid, self-satisfied air all their devoted gallants display, that would be the end of it, for me."

One of M. Brisse's lunges almost touched him, but Angelo disposed of it with his usual brilliance. The only concession he made was to deprive himself of his former rambles in the pine woods. He developed a habit, after every bout, of strolling for an hour or so under the tall trees and then riding back to Aix at a walking pace, with the ladies' carriages bowling along beside him.

The little theatre, which gave a weekly performance of Rossini and Mozart, opened every Saturday night. The artistes came from Marseilles by coach during the course of the afternoon. The prima donna was always feted by all the gentlemen, but she singled no one out for any special favour. Her most zealous suitor was Lacroix-Plainval, a young first lieutenant, dark and vivacious, who seemed to be a sort of catering officer. She often passed by the Prytaneum while Angelo was away in the pine woods, but this time she saw him walking under the trees. "Call that boy over to see me," said she. "I would not dare to call him," replied Lacroix-Plainval. "What a fool I should look if he replied that he was not kicking his heels till I happened to want him. But, if you like, I will go and ask him to come." "What a fuss you make over a trifle," she replied.

"Don't you see that kicking his heels is just what he's doing?" Without standing on ceremony she called to him herself, and a moment later he had joined the company in the arbour.

"We have all found you most intriguing," Lacroix-Plainval remarked to him. "Obviously you have been a soldier. I noticed that you finish all your wide sweeping strokes with a little outward twist to right or left, like a man accustomed to avoiding his horse's ears."

"My background is simple in the extreme, Lieutenant," Angelo replied. "I am the son of a priest. The periods my mother spent with her father confessor were a trifle too intimate. He was a good *curé* of Savoy (a man of excellent family, too,) and when I was ten she entrusted me to him so that he could have me educated. But in my country, which is Savoy, a churchman's bastard has to put up with ribald taunts from the common people. It even happens, sometimes, that our worthy peasants, jealous of the fact that we can read, vent their spite on us with cudgels. I learned to use arms by practising with a retired cavalry sergeant who possessed only two swords. I was determined to learn how to beat off any attack from a cudgel, or at least to get my own back with a certain elegance. I object to being laughed at." He volunteered his little story with perfect gravity and an air of natural candour. "I love dare-devils," Anna Clèves murmured in his ear. "Come to my dressing-room this evening." He duly took her at her word. She was a woman of thirty with a good deal of experience, but she perceived that she did not have enough.

"This damned face of mine," said Angelo to himself looking at his reflection in the mirrors. There was nothing the poor woman could find to do, except to go on languidly powdering her breasts, which were very beautiful and justly celebrated. She sang *In te la fed' e la bontà del core* without lifting her eyes from the spot where Angelo had taken his seat in the stalls. The theatre was very small and everyone in the audience noticed it.

"I ought to do something to please Mme Hortense," he thought to himself, and one Saturday he told Anna Clèves about the little door in the garden. "Is the caretaker's lodge at the Bishop's palace open after midnight?" she immediately asked. He had not given it a thought. "I do not know," said he. "Go and open it," she answered. The problem of what happened at the Bishop's house after midnight caused Angelo considerable uncertainty. He crossed the broad corridor of the porter's lodge with infinite precautions, and took at least five minutes to undo the bolts of the door giving on to the narrow street. No sooner had he opened it than Anna Clèves threw her arms around him. "I've been waiting for half an hour," she told him, her voice broken by little sobs as she showered him with kisses. "I heard all the trouble you had with the bolts. But if you hadn't managed to open the door, I made up my mind I would throw stones in at the porter's window and pacify him with some tale or other, or even by paying him," and she tapped Angelo with a little chain-mesh purse she carried in her hand. "What sort of plaster has she put on her face?" he was wondering to himself. "My mouth is as dusty as if it were carnival time." He did not like her little purse, either.

He brought her through the gardens and, once in his rooms, he took some time to light six candles in their stands. "And now, what?" he said to himself. In the end, he managed to carry it off with perfect chivalry. "What a pity that love-making does not appeal to you," she said. "No," she added, placing her fingers over his lips, "do not lie to me. It's no good your telling me little stories like the one about your being the son of a priest. Just say nothing, and I will be your friend." There was no longer any touch of the theatre about her. As she spoke of friendship she was completely natural, her voice was wistful, and a tear slipped down to the corner of her quivering mouth. "Even if you are not in love," she was able to say at last, "you need someone to love you. There is much prejudice against a woman of my profession, but I am not as bad as people say. In any case, I value tenderness above everything, and if you will sometimes stroke my hair as you are doing now, I shall thank heaven for it every night of my life." Deeply moved by her manifest sincerity, Angelo was indeed caressing her hair and even her tiny ears. He, too, was sincere in his response, and managed to find a few words that made her delirious with joy. "This is the most wonderful night of my life," she told him. "We must be careful not to spoil it. Next Saturday, instead of sharing the *berline* with the rest of the troupe, I will come by the stagecoach from Arles, and will be at your little door by ten in the morning. Let me stay an hour here with you while you finish dressing. These rooms need to be lived in, now and then, by a woman who loves you, even by me, though I mean nothing to you." And her eyes were wild. "Towards noon we will set out for Saint-Antonin, where there is a little inn you will like, and country that will charm your heart. We will stroll there like good friends. I must make sure of giving you happy times to remember, since I cannot give you anything else," and her tears fell upon Angelo's hands.

"In that event," he reflected, "I shall be obliged to forego my fencing bouts one day a week. It's to be hoped that the countryside is as lovely as she says it is."

It was even lovelier, and reminded him of landscapes in Tuscany. It was almost impossible to gaze unmoved at the gently undulating skyline, where infinitely noble green-bronze waves rolled away under immense clouds whose dazzling beauty was tinged with sadness. Anna was mounted on a mare from a riding school, and rode well. Angelo had carefully tried out the animal beforehand, anxious to avoid the risk of any mishap that might cause him endless embarrassment.

The inn was deserted until three o'clock in the afternoon. The shutters had been closed against the fierce sunlight. The room was vast and cool. The courtyard had been sprinkled with water and smelt of clay. Anna and Angelo sat in two armchairs, facing each other. Three insignificant men came in without a sound.

"These clothes of mine are not practical," was Angelo's first thought. "I could not bring my dagger with me, and I shall have to wrestle with these fellows like a carter if this fair lady means to avenge the minor affront I gave her the other night." The men went across to the back of the room, which lay in shadow. There came a sound of cases being opened. Anna seemed lost in a dream. Then a violin, a viola and a flute began to play the heartbreaking *andante* from Mozart's *Concerto in C.*

Anna had to get ready for the evening's performance, so they were obliged to return early. Angelo paid the musicians royally. "The world I have lived in makes it difficult for me, alas, to be familiar with what goes on in ordinary life. The one is so far removed from the other. But," he said to her, "I do not believe what happened just now came about by chance. What gives you the insight to discover the very things my heart most needs?"

"It is simply that I love you," she replied, "and that I am a fool. Then one can devise all sorts of things, like God. I assure you, this is the first pleasure I have found in my misfortune. However, I am no goddess sprung from Jupiter's thigh. I was a dressmaker in Marseilles until an impresario, who was my mother's lover, then mine, agreed to spend a little money on having my voice trained. But I am sure that,

for you, I can easily think as nobly as any high-born lady."
"What she tells me is most moving," Angelo thought to
himself. "How can I manage to thank her? I certainly am
not in love."

"May it be that I am incapable of loving?" he pondered
when he was once more alone at home. He had spent the
whole day roaming in the country with Anna, asking himself every moment whether he was really doing all he could
to make his companion happy. The same landscape came
again before his eyes and filled the four walls of his room
like a subtly lighted *décor*. "Had I been with the woman so
truly made for me that the perfume she devised holds
everything I want from life, this would have been paradise,"
he mused. "Even if she were ugly. Even if she were an
invalid, borne on a litter drawn by two horses. What intimate trains of thought we could have shared, inspired by
these magnificent clouds, these hills rolling away as far as
the eye can see, like the waves of the ocean!"

There were other outings to Saint-Augustin. He began
to notice that the Mont Sainte-Victoire looked like a great
sailing ship with all sails set, but he kept this piece of
imagery to himself. "What would she make of it?" he questioned. "In any case, I'm a long way from my swordplay,
here. Would it perhaps be better for me to make myself
a foreman?" He was utterly serious about it, and had almost
made up his mind to go and see the Tyrolean in his wooden
hut when he received a little note from the Vicar-General
begging him to come. It was Rosette who brought it
to him. The whole affair seemed an intervention of
Providence, even the young girl who stood waiting rather
sheepishly, rolling up her apron and making eyes at him. At
last she was indiscreet enough to say: "I think he needs you
for something," in a tone that conveyed a hint of equality.
Angelo whistled as he dressed.

"I took the liberty of sending for you," said the Vicar-General, "and I am rather troubled because all I have to tell you is something you may find childish. I am afraid it may give you a poor opinion of me. I have been pining for you. That is the sole reason for my clumsy advances. It is almost a month since I last saw you. I miss you, though I ought not to tell you so." He went on talking for five minutes or more about his lack of discretion. Angelo responded at almost equal length with extravagant protestations of affection. "If you talk to me like that," said the Vicar, "how do you expect me to keep calm? Today, let us talk man to man. I have shown you quite frankly that I am much attached to the good things of life. This place is by no means a monk's cell. Besides, the fact is that, in military parlance, my generals have thought fit to use me as a soldier in the world at large. I shall always remember telling a certain priest – when I was your age – 'I am very susceptible to temptations, Father, and you are putting me in a position where they will give me no peace.' 'Learn to avail yourself of compromise,' he advised me. 'He was a saint, I don't know why it is that so far no miracles have taken place in a blaze of glory over his bones. I'm telling you all this because my courage fails me, and I'm beating about the bush. We have been on friendly terms, but that is no longer enough to satisfy me. I have resisted this yearning, but these past few weeks, when you seemed to be neglecting me, have made me see very plainly how vain it is to resist a temptation of this sort. And since, following my saint's advice, I have made it a habit to be satisfied with a compromise, this is what I propose. There is no question of anything that would tie you, merely a simple tacit agreement between us, and your heart will immediately tell you whether you could accept. Will you be my son?

It would mean that henceforward we should share each other's interests, and you would freely give me the right to intervene in your life as a father would. If you need to think it over, do not answer at once."

The Vicar-General had expressed himself without the least emotion. Angelo, deeply moved, let his heart speak. "That's fine, then," said the Vicar. "Naturally there is no question of filial devotion. There is hardly enough difference in our ages for that, and if it were not for my cassock and this premature ageing that comes from a professional study of human wickedness it would be utterly ridiculous for me to imagine myself father to a colonel. You appreciate there's no need to call me Papa. Let us just be comrades until the moment comes – and I doubt whether it ever will – when I want you to become my Cid Campeador. For my part, of course, I shall act towards you as a father to his son. The only token of affection I ask is that you realise this, and make full use of me. Do you need money?"

"There will never be any question of that," Angelo retorted. His quick resentment made the Vicar-General smile. "You must quite understand," said he, "that I was not trying to probe or ask for proofs."

"I was not thinking of giving you any," said Angelo dryly, chilled by his companion's smile.

"Always correct me like that if I am tactless," the Vicar-General replied, "and I shall be infinitely obliged to you. And now, a question that has been burning my lips ever since you came in and I looked on your face again. Why do I see no happiness in your eyes?"

"My days are empty and time hangs heavily," Angelo answered him. "A hundred years from now, when national unity is a recognised fact and States are built on a sound constitution, I very much wonder what men like me will do to avoid boredom. The best moment of my life was spent in killing the Baron. You will grant it was all too short . . . When you sent for me I was seriously thinking of taking service with those compatriots of mine who still feel passionately enthusiastic."

"Take good care you do not," said the Vicar. "You would have to go back to Piedmont, which is, after all, only a narrow strip of a country, between the mountains and the sea. It has been big enough for you till now, but there are vaster arenas for games of chance, and those are the ones you will yearn for when your hand of *bouillotte* on that little card table is finished. How will you get along with the Ministry that your grateful monarchy will set up under your very nose? What will happen when you stand before the magistrate's chair in the phalanstery that your generous friends will build, if the worst comes to the worst, over the scaffold of the House of Savoy? The zeal, the passions I discern in you, cannot be satisfied merely by national unity. So far, let us admit it, the world of politics has given you an outlet, but it cannot go on doing so indefinitely. You are an individualist. Such men always have one close friend, never more." With supreme diplomacy he went on without a pause to speak of the Duchess Ezzia, as though her name came naturally to his lips. "Territories may be thrown together by the tricks of statecraft," he added, "but only passionate zeal can weld them into a nation."

"There, my heart!" Angelo said to himself. "You were mad to think you could hold yourself in check with a little sword and an opera singer. Even with the corpse of an informer."

"You had to begin with something," the Vicar continued, seeming to read his thoughts, "and everything has its use. That is one of the great laws of life. So open your heart to me as a son should. That is how our contract can be of service."

"Nothing could be simpler," said Angelo. "I, for my part, cannot be satisfied with compromise. That is the whole truth of the matter. I have none of your weighty reasons for giving up the substance and choosing the shadow. Ought I to think up some such reason for myself? And join in the labours of those fanatical navvies as a foreman?"

"Let us not talk shop," said the Vicar. "The root of the matter lies deeper than that. It was not for nothing that, the other day, I made you look at yourself full length in my wardrobe mirror. A man's spirit can do him more harm than tobacco or coffee. You wear a scapular of Saint Januarius, and that's a perfectly good thing to do. But you also wear another scapular – not sanctified, I imagine – and unless I am mistaken, I think that is going rather beyond perfection. Do not be surprised that I know these details. Put it down to my tender care for you. Mme Hortense, I assure you, keeps a secret buried from all the world, except from me. I will not conceal from you any longer that ever since I came to love you I have been anxious about you, and I instructed her to help me, for your own good. She caught sight of these two symbols an evening or two ago, when you were enjoying the cool freshness of the garden, with your shirt open."

"Would he be a Jesuit?" Angelo debated in his mind. "In any case, I shall beware of Mme Hortense, and if ever she comes burrowing in my shirt again I shall make her blush to such good purpose that she will never dare to carry any more tittle tattle to this worthy man. I understand your feelings," he continued aloud. "It was stiflingly hot that night. Still, there was no need for that good woman to violate her modesty to the extent of peering inside my open-necked shirt. Your affection for me, especially now there is something paternal about it, and my own feeling toward you, will ensure that I have absolutely nothing to conceal from you. But let us begin at the beginning. There is no need, I suppose, for me to tell you of my intrigue with this opera singer?"

"None whatever," said the Vicar amiably. "No one buys a halfpenny worth of writing paper in Aix without my knowing the watermark of the paper and the quality of the gum on the envelope. My knowledge of details that concern you is even more comprehensive. I know, for instance, that now and then drunken men bump into you in deserted alleyways, and that, so far, you have escaped without injury from these brief contacts. I know, too, that Mme Clèves quite often arranges little private concerts for you, and during one of the most recent you asked the musicians to play for you a little piece by Brahms, called, I believe, *Regrets*. So you can speak freely."

"Well now," thought Angelo, "what else is there to say?"

"There are, however, several things left for you to tell me," continued the Vicar, who seemed to read him like an open book. "In particular, what goes on in your heart. I have plenty of information to convince me that you are not in love, and you yourself confirmed it to me just now. But is that due to the lady, or to you?"

"He's talking just as she does," said Angelo to himself. "Why do they have to ask me: 'Do you like love, my boy?' Of course I do." But he was troubled by the questions he had already asked himself on that subject. "Ought I to tell him about the kerchief? If I did, he would certainly laugh at me. This man is the devil himself. But I did kill the Baron. And Heaven knows how many times I have galloped all night long, to spend a couple of hours in a mountain cave with men who kept their faces hidden and told me a hundred things, one of which would have been enough to hang an entire regiment!" He was so disconcerted by the realisation that he had almost told this cold, perspicacious man about the perfumed handkerchief, that he was obliged to pull himself together. At last he became aware that his silence was growing too prolonged to be attributed simply to an anxiety that his reply should be explicit.

"I will be frank," he told the Vicar. "With me, nothing counts unless my heart is in it. And I am very hard to please. Though the women you have here are surrounded by fountains worthy of Rome, plane trees like those of Greece and a sky portraying the tragedy of Don Quixote at every street corner, I shall never love them. I am perhaps incapable of getting outside myself, but unless people will come and seek me out on my own ground, they will never meet me at all. Until someone does, I while away my time smoking. Maybe it is Madame Clèves I inhale . . ." He was rather pleased with these little figures of speech that fear had helped him find. "Hide yourself deep in my inmost soul, lovely fragrance," he was saying. "This demon shall never know of you."

"But," the Vicar replied, "suppose you were to meet a *rara avis*? Then I can well imagine you tossing aside the rest of your cigar. Would you always be as firm in your determination not to compromise?"

"Certainly," said Angelo. "The moment would be now or never. So much so that I should probably manage to keep the substance as well as the shadow."

"One of these days," observed the Vicar-General, "I think I may ask you to do me a little service."

They fell to gossiping of trivial matters till they were both in fits of laughter. "Stay to supper," said the Vicar. "I have taught Rosette the invaluable habit of always having one of her 'impromptus' ready. I should be very surprised if she hasn't a cold fowl to set before us." Eventually Angelo returned home very late, and in high good humour.

7

It was some time since his last visit to the Vicar-General when, on a certain autumn evening, as night was rapidly closing in from a sky that threatened rain, Angelo went for a stroll through the more outlying quarters of the town to savour a mood of pleasurable melancholy and enjoy the smell of dead leaves.

He had paused under the dim red light of a street-lamp, when a man came forward from the shadows of some tall elms and said to him: "You seem very deep in thought, my dear colonel!" It was the man in the cape. "I have been watching you for a moment," he went on. "You looked exactly as though you were waiting at a rendezvous. I can't resist nocturnal trysts. But if I am in your way . . ."

"There's no question of that at all," said Angelo. "I only came out to listen to the sound of the wind, and to be alone. But there is no one whose company I would rather have than yours. I should be delighted if you would come home with me."

"Then I will, if it is not too far, and if I can leave in a couple of hours without anyone seeing me," replied the other.

"You can even come in without being seen," said Angelo, and he brought him through the Rue Caisserie.

"Wait a minute, my young friend," said the man in the cape, when he saw they were entering the passage leading to the porter's lodge. "Would you be playing games with me? This is the Archbishop's residence."

Angelo made him touch the door in the passage wall that gave on to the lilac trees of his garden. He pushed it, they passed through tunnels of jasmine which at that time of the year smelt like a wet dog, and went up to his rooms.

"This is providential," said the man in the cape, and while Angelo was lighting the candles he went over to the windows. "Do you happen to have a telescope? Look! I imagine the light I can see down there is coming from one of the Archbishop's private rooms. Doubtless behind those window panes he is in the midst of his evening devotions. I am a monster of curiosity! What wouldn't I give to catch a glimpse of a prostrate archbishop! You haven't a telescope, of course? That would be too much to hope for. Had I only known, I would have brought one. It's impossible to think of everything. But what's been happening to you since we were on the road to Peyrolles? At any rate you've turned into an extremely elegant young man!"

In a few words Angelo described his life in Aix, but without mentioning the Vicar. He felt his companion would probably laugh at that churchman's appeal to him for filial affection. "You are the one I've been worrying about for some time," he said. "That coachman was off his head and led us a hellish dance. When I made him pull up at the top of the hill, I heard pistol shots coming from the place where I left you."

"There were a few shots," said the man. "Four or five; nothing to speak of. The whole affair was over like a flash, a hundred yards away from where I was, and though there was a moon all I could see was a scrimmage. There was no point in my sticking my nose in. Would you be very kind," he went on abruptly, "and let us blow out the candles? The lighted window in the Archbishop's palace looks like a bright eye watching us. It makes me restless. We haven't a telescope, but they may have. I have a shocking habit of picking my nose when anyone tells me an interesting story, and I should not like His Lordship to know about that. For you are going to tell me something interesting, I am sure.

Besides, I am anti-clerical. Blow out the candles, my young friend, let us stay in the dark."

Angelo, highly entertained by all this, blew out the candles. His bout of depression had vanished. He half opened the drawer where he kept his dagger.

"Come and sit beside me, near the window. If anyone comes in and asks you who I am, I am an astronomer friend of yours, giving you a lecture on the stars."

"No one comes in here to ask me questions," Angelo replied, "and besides, there are no stars. The sky is overcast and it is going to rain."

"1 have underestimated you," said the other. "Shrewd observations, and quite unanswerable. Then would you have any objection if, while we go on chatting in this friendly fashion, I cast my eye, now and then, on the episcopal window? It intrigues me so much."

"You are my guest," Angelo replied, "and I think highly enough of you to feel confident you would do nothing discreditable here."

"A special candle should be lit before the portrait of your mother who has brought you up so well! Not to mention your innate nobility. 'Discreditable'! Marvellous! You are ermine personified! And now, to the heart of the matter. Did you see the old wolf?"

"What old wolf is that?"

"Come on, now! Tell me how you restored that provoking woman to her family, and I will point out the wolf to you as we go along."

"Do you mean the Marquise?"

"Herself, and her brother."

"They were extremely kind." Angelo gave a circumstantial account of his clashes with the coachman, the pleasant misunderstanding at the inn, his reception at the chateau in the afternoon.

"You scatterbrain!" exclaimed the man in the cape. "You did not do as I told you. I said: 'Do not leave her till she is at her door.' I always mean exactly what I say. You should not have let them put you down at the inn. Her door was right up on the terrace, and that's where you should have gone. You ought to have escorted her to that door and said to the lackey with the habitual air of command that I imagine a colonel can always adopt: 'I wish to place Madame in the care of her brother personally.' Any such high and mighty phrase spoken late at night, on a threshold overlooking a park, by a man of your quality to a sleepy, listless manservant, would have produced the results I was counting on. Then you could have given me a careful report of them today. I had no time to explain all that to you while we were under the oak, but I was banking on your punctilious courtesy to a lady."

Angelo was not in the least ruffled by the heated tone of these reproaches. He found it all rather charming. "What a lover!" he thought to himself. "To be so solicitous at fifty years of age, and for a woman of more than sixty, fully capable of commanding respect in hell itself! I did not think," he said aloud, "that the Marquise could run into any grave danger between the inn and the chateau."

"Not the slightest," replied the other calmly. "But you would have been able to tell me whether the old wolf was at home that night. As it turns out, you don't know."

"I know he was home the next day, at any rate," Angelo returned.

"The next day, everyone was at home," said the man in the cape, "except two police officers. That's no longer either here nor there."

"Would you suspect the Marquise of holding up a stagecoach?" laughed Angelo.

"I do not suspect anyone," the man replied hastily. "It is

not my business to suspect. I have no right to suspect. You misunderstand my interest. Yes, what I meant to talk about was the two gendarmes who were killed. They, in point of fact, are the only men who didn't go home and stay there, on the day when the Marquis, too, was at home. But do not draw any conclusions from that except that I love the drama of passing events and exciting subjects for conversation."

Angelo was entranced by the darkness, the mystery, the half-open drawer where his dagger lay, the night wind, the evasive reticence of this romantic fellow. He was thoroughly enjoying the evening. "What you need, my French friend," he said good-humouredly, "is an Austria. You have no such national enemy, so you are obliged to invent little piecemeal revolts by secret societies like our *carbonari*, to provide you with some diversion. The funniest thing is that the old wolf had his own suspicions about you. He openly told me he thought you might belong to the police."

"The devil he did!" exclaimed the man in the cape. "How very irritating!"

"It was all well within the bounds of polite conversation."

"It is precisely when I think of polite conversation that I find these suspicions very awkward. They force me to change my plans. I meant to go and call on that obstinate lady. But what sort of figure should I cut now?"

"The same as you do here tonight, and that is by no means displeasing. An air of intrigue suits you very well."

"Unfortunately, during such a visit I should have to keep intrigue out of my thoughts as strictly as ropes are banned from the home of a man who has been hanged. I wanted to turn myself fairly and squarely out to grass, and spend pleasant hours in relaxation and mutual confidences."

"There's the *bourgeois* type of mind showing itself again," thought Angelo to himself. "The Marquise," he went on, "seemed to attach no importance whatever to the discussion, and the Marquis himself showed complete indifference to what, after all, was said merely to while away a boring afternoon of heavy rain under the shelter of tall trees. (I had better not tell him," he reflected, "that the Marquis was taking the affair as seriously as he was himself a moment ago. These little Frenchmen are really funny with their sterile secret societies. Now we, when we are hunting out conspirators, at least have the good sense to cast our nets wide enough not to entangle our own legs.) Do I need to assure you," he continued aloud, "that neither I nor anyone else could take these suspicions seriously?"

"Do you really think so?" enquired the man in the cape, and his voice had no answering tone of banter.

"What a *frousse*!" thought Angelo, using one of M. Brisse's slang words for a fuss about nothing. "Don't you know," he said, "the dismal grey of rain in these houses over-topped by great trees? It gets dark there by three o'clock in the afternoon. You have to sprinkle salt on every word to give any taste at all to your conversation. The event of the night before was a godsend, and they talked about you as they would have talked about the Grand Turk."

Though the night was very dark, the face of the man in the cape was sharply outlined against the grey panes. His eyes were turned towards the Archbishop's window, where a lamp was still burning. Suddenly it went out.

"Here we've got it!" said the man in the cape, starting to his feet. "I must be off. How long does it take to go from this room to your garden door, taking all the usual precautions?"

"One minute."

"Then I still have one left. Just long enough to give you a strict command. This time, take it seriously. Do not speak of me or my visit to a living soul. That is vitally important. I told you to keep silent once before, and you took no notice. Still, I bear you no grudge on that account. You could not muzzle the Marquise. That is beyond the power of any human being. Today, you have no one to control but yourself. I charge you on your honour, hold your tongue."

"More blood-curdling romance!" Angelo thought to himself. "What fun he is having!" He did not feel in the least inclined to take offence at the other's tone of command when speaking of his honour. "So that you can see how well I understand the gravity of the affair," he said, "I would have you know that I have often brought women home with me through that secret door. So if you will hide your face in your coat collar, ruffle out your hair, show your buckled shoes and take little mincing steps, anyone we might be unlucky enough to meet in the shadows of the garden would think it perfectly natural for us to be walking there. Come along."

"You're not short of good ideas," said the man in the cape, with the utmost seriousness.

Shortly before the lamp in the Archbishop's window was extinguished, the Vicar-General was standing beside it, preparing to take his leave. The Archbishop was nursing the early stages of an attack of gout in this little room where the rustling of the trees helped him to sleep.

"You haven't made up your mind?" the Archbishop enquired.

"I do not believe in the solidarity of any alliance between the nobility of the old regime and the clergy," replied the Vicar-General. "I do not even see any need for it."

"Do not generalise. Tell me what is in your heart. What have you got against the Marquis?"

"I must use one more generalisation to make my thought clear to you. They can't stand ridicule; we know how to put up with it and turn it to our advantage. What they are really fighting against is any recurrence of '93; we are so convinced that what happened in the Year of the Terror will happen again, that we are already thoroughly prepared for it."

"Alliance does not mean suicide. One ally invariably dies before the other. That is only natural."

"They are losing their privileges and we are keeping ours. How can you expect them to love us?"

"As for expecting them to love us, there is the question of services rendered, and that was arranged long ago. You have good eyes. Count me out ten drops of colchium in this glass. What is it that you have against the Marquis? His daring?"

"His romantic ideas."

"Seven hundred thousand francs in six months."

"His rashness."

"He is shrewd. We are even shrewder."

"His fundamental error."

"I know. But one of the most awkward problems in the preparation of civil war is that it demands even more mental concentration to know what not to tell one's friends than to decide what action to take against one's enemies."

"We are not capable of tearing up paving stones ourselves. Barricades are not built for a fixed price. His error is that he believes they are. Seven hundred thousand francs in six months merely means seven hundred thousand francs on the one hand, and six months wasted on the other."

"What would you have done in those six months?"

"I should have opened hostilities with weapons familiar to us, while M. de Théus firmly expects the fighting to start with weapons we shall never know how to use. The public does not rise in revolt out of dire necessity, but out of passion. Therein lies the secret behind Blanqui's persecution, the secret of Barbès, Martin Bernard, and the 12th of May, the exaltation a man feels on being condemned to death, especially when the penalty is commuted. What would you do with seven hundred thousand francs, or even with two million, when the feelings of the mob are running high? Are you counting on the nobles? All they know is how to die. That defines them exactly. The real treasure in any revolution is time. M. de Théus is filling our coffers but costing us time. In six months it would be possible to create and foster an enthusiasm in quite the opposite sense."

"Do you propose doing that?" asked the Archbishop.

"Not personally. I am in excellent health this evening. If I had taken a dose of opium for my rheumatism I should doubtless have said yes. But I could have blamed it on the medicine."

"What are you afraid of? We appreciate a good intention just as much as success."

"I do not doubt that, but I have a congenital aversion to honorary 'associate-members'."

"Possibly we can obtain firm promises, simply out of good will. M. de Théus has already given us more than promises."

"My shooting pains usually start when we have heavy rain," observed the Vicar-General. "It looks like rain tonight. It is possible that I may take a little opium at the end of next week. Your attack of gout will probably be over by then?"

"I hardly think so. It seems likely to persist. I find these affairs very troublesome. But there is nothing to hinder you from coming to see me. Your rheumatism is in your arm, I think?"

"My right arm, my lord."

"The right? Oh! So that will prevent any written undertakings, I gather. Anyway, it is not on the same side as your heart, that's the most important thing. We must always find some way to render thanks to Providence. Moreover, we will never discard M. de Théus. What he is doing is so chivalrous! He's like a knight of the Middle Ages. If he is to break with us, the suggestion must come from him. Unless, of course, his resignation were provoked by treacheries. If a train of clues were to fall into the hands of certain inquisitive people there is no knowing where it would lead. You are constantly in touch with the Marquis, I believe?"

"Constantly, my lord. Have no fear. I shall not attack M. de Théus from any angle that might involve us all. But he could have trouble at home. His wife is very young."

"The colchium is making me sleepy. I think you should attach no importance to anything I say. That's not a bad idea of yours."

"I will let you rest. Before I have my attack of rheumatism, do you think I might present to you a young friend of mine who would particularly value your blessing?"

"I am dropping asleep," said the Archbishop. "Goodnight. Blow out the lamp. Yes, bring him."

"Goodnight, my lord."

The Vicar-General blew out the lamp and left the room.

8

SCARCELY HAD ANGELO LEFT the chateau of La Vallette when the Marquise of Théus said to her brother: "I have come more than thirty leagues, I nearly had my throat cut, I found myself in a compromising situation with that young scamp to whom you have lent one of your best horses that you will never see again. You wrote to tell me you were married; I came to see your wife; and all I do is to keep your out-of-work bishop company or look out at your copper beeches, and you know they are trees I detest. What is behind all this? Have you married some devilish creature? Does she appear in clouds of sulphurous smoke, and you fear my health would not stand it? Is she out of her mind? Are we waiting for her to recover from some fit or other? Or is she badly brought up, so that you are afraid of what I shall think? Is she a baboon? Are you ashamed for the first time in your life? In short, what is wrong? Where is she? Is she an intelligent woman? Has she left you already?"

Two days later, Pauline arrived, wearing a simple riding habit. "Why! She's as charming as a fawn," said the Marquise in amazement. She contrived to meet her alone in the great corridor on the first floor. The young woman, humming to herself as she came, gave a start as the Marquise surged forth from the window embrasure, but at once broke into a smile.

"Let me look at you," said the Marquise. "But you are all eyes! Who gave you such a tiny face for those great eyes?"

"My father," said the girl. "I take after him, apparently."

"That's a lie," exclaimed the Marquise. "No man could be capable of it. It must be your mother."

"I never knew her," the girl replied. "She died when I was born."

"I can understand that," said the Marquise. "Contentment and rest. I should have done just the same. Ah, well! If she gave you her wisdom, too, you will be closer to my heart than any human being I have ever known."

"Closer even than Diablon," she said to herself as she entered her own room. It was three o'clock in the afternoon and the sun was oppressive, making a siesta doubly inviting, but the Marquise did not uncover her bed. She took off her shoes and stockings and walked barefoot on the cool tiles. "If I were her mother," she said aloud, "I should mount guard over her with a gun. I should watch over her as she slept. And I should have given her a good smack or two on her wedding morning." For more than an hour she scoffed at her own feelings. She could not believe her good fortune.

"How old are you?" she asked her a little later. "Twenty-two." They were in the library waiting for the gong to sound for dinner, seated side by side upon a *bergère*, facing the wide window that looked out over the park. The Marquise had been caressing the hand of her young companion, but now let it lie still. The joy it gave her was too poignant. "Are you happy?" she asked.

"Very happy," replied the girl, her voice serene.

"And that's the truth," the Marquise said to herself. "That voice holds no guile. In her eyes I can see the still reflection of a tree standing at least a hundred yards away on the far side of the lawn. It is the absolute truth."

As soon as dinner was over the Marquise went up to her room, eager to be alone with her discovery. "She is a child," she said to herself. She could still feel that soft little hand slipping into her own. "How strange life can be! Everything led me to believe that all I could count on, henceforth, was keeping a few memories and using no little artifice to make the best of a bad job, and to my utter amazement I discover a child. I have not seen a single gesture or glance, nor heard a single word, that is not a child's gesture, glance or word. Even her grave carefulness not to seem like a child, is childish. She has dressed her hair in a low chignon like a fine lady as though she were playing a game. Everything about her is candid, pure and full of peace. Her heart is as clear as water. I do not even know if her eyes have any colour . . . all I can see is their sincerity. Laurent is eight years older than I am, almost nine. What other follies will he commit in the few years he has yet to live? The consequences of any wild schemes of his shall not fall upon this child, if I can help it. I will set my affairs in order. If he dies, I want her to live with me. Théus is mine. And hers." She was overwhelmed with joy to think she once more loved someone alive.

There was a little tap on her door and Pauline came in, wearing a long nightdress. "May I talk to you?" she asked.

"Do not walk barefoot on the cold tiles," said the Marquise. "Come on the carpet and put this shawl around your shoulders. Or, better still, lie down in my bed where you will be warm and comfortable. I will sit in the armchair. Wait, I will bolt the door," she went on, wild with delight.

"I am not cold," laughed Pauline. "I love walking barefoot in my nightdress."

For several minutes the Marquise, utterly beside herself, breathlessly scolded her, tenderly imagining all the draughts, the countless risks of illness that might threaten her treasure. In the end Pauline, covered with cloaks and her feet wrapped in shawls, sat in an armchair at the head of the bed where she had obliged the Marquise to lie down.

"You asked me whether I was happy," she said, "and that

is why I came to see you. I have sometimes been asked that question, and I know it is because my husband is almost fifty years older than I am."

At the word "husband", it seemed to the Marquise that her candles went out, only to shine forth again upon a world she had not foreseen. "That's true," she thought, "and only this afternoon I was saying to myself that if I had been her mother I would have given her a smack or two on her wedding morning. But I was imagining a marriage still to come, not one already in being, and, above all, I was not thinking of Laurent."

"I told my friends," Pauline went on, "that I was very happy, for those girls were the first to ask me. But I did not tell them why. I am too proud for that. If you are wondering about my happiness, I must explain that it took me a long time to realise why I was asked that question. As soon as I understood, I asked Laurent's permission to go and reassure my father. What was mere curiosity in other people, could have been real anxiety for him. I went to tell him my reasons, and that was what deprived me of the pleasure of welcoming you on your arrival. You have been so kind to me from the first, you are so different from the spiteful, jealous women I have met, your face is so much like that of my old nurse who brought me up and used to rock me to sleep, that tonight, when you asked me the question I have come to expect, I wanted to embrace you and reassure you as I did my father."

It must be confessed that the Marquise literally burst into tears. "Come to my heart," she sobbed. "You are an angel. Ah! Why did you marry my brother?"

"Because I love him," said the girl, clasping the Marquise in her arms. Without realising it, the Marquise had regarded Pauline as if she were her niece. She was still trying hard to convince herself that Laurent was the man in question when she heard this declaration of love. The quick movement Pauline made to lean over the bed, displaced the cloak and uncovered the apples of her breasts. "Cover yourself up," said the Marquise severely. "You must not do anything rash that could cause endless harm. The nights are chilly and you are just at the age when you might get consumption."

She pushed her away, made her sit down again, and with her own hands fastened round the young girl's neck the collar of the astrakhan cape she had thrown across her shoulders. "Would you like me to leave you now?" asked Pauline, somewhat abashed.

"Certainly not," said the Marquise, "I do not want you to catch cold, that's all. So you have reassured your father with reasons that must be good. Well, now you must reassure your mother. I warn you, that will be much more difficult."

"You are even better than I dared hope," Pauline told her. "I knew his sister must possess the same qualities that he has, but you have the advantage of not hiding your goodness. We are more soft-hearted," said she with an artlessness that once more brought a flood of tears that the Marquise did not wipe from her eyes.

"Do not try to get round me," the Marquise managed to say, her mouth trembling. "I am going to be very severe, for it is your happiness that will depend on this question."

"Have you ever been lost in a dream?" asked the girl.

"I have never done anything else," the Marquise replied, slipping her hand through the cloak to touch Pauline's arm. "Am I dreaming now?" she asked herself.

"Then everything will be easy to understand," said Pauline. "But first I must tell you who I am, for you do not know. Ten leagues from here is a fairly large market town called Rians, and it is there that my father practises as a doctor. He is a kindly man, always preoccupied with matters outside his own personal interest. Everyone loves him. At all events, no one would dare to say they did not. But because he gives his services free to people who cannot pay, I do not think they greatly respect him. Moreover, his blue eyes are so clear that their glance always seems mild and one might well imagine that in thought he is far away from the place where he actually is. This has greatly encouraged the lack of respect with which everyone treats him, especially the peasants of the neighbourhood, who are well aware of what a sou is worth, and despise anything that cannot be valued in that fashion. He has a further characteristic that makes him seem alien to the place where he lives, where, indeed, we were both born. It is that when danger threatens – in his work as a doctor, of course, for he has no other dangers to face – he has remarkable precision, a will of iron, even, when necessary, a ruthlessness that nothing can resist. I understand the local people very well, and do not blame them. It must be most painful to be forced to obey for your very life a man you do not respect, whose gaze you consider too limpid and guileless. But he has helped three quarters of the population of Rians into the world, and, too, has effected five or six cures that could easily pass for miracles."

"Do not tell me any more about your father. Tell me of your mother who is dead," said the Marquise naively. She was jealous. "Come!" she said to herself. "Must I resign myself to hearing still more about who-knows-what from this silly little thing? She loves everybody. Just now it was Laurent, now it is her father. If she imagines I shall have any truck with that sort of company, she is much mistaken. Well then," she went on aloud, "talk of anybody you like, but I would rather it was someone you do not love, or at least someone who has been dead a long time, like your mother."

"You shall at least understand why I was swept off my feet," said Pauline rather shrewdly. "A little more than a year ago, my father and I were riding home through the wood of La Gardiole during a violent thunderstorm; in the torrent and already half-drowned, we found a man who was wounded in the shoulder."

"That's a bit too much," said the Marquise. "Precisely where is your father going to find all that? I cannot do with men who are wounded and drowned at the same time. I simply want – do you understand, my girl? – to hear a little more about things that accord with your lovely great eyes. Still, I can see from your obstinate forehead that in the end you will polish me off with heaven knows how many men who have been wounded, drowned, broken on the wheel, hanged from the yard arm, quartered and boiled. Get along with you! Your man was wounded in the shoulder, you say?"

"By a shot."

"And over and above that, he was drowned?"

"Only half drowned. He was lying on the steep river bank and his legs were already floating in the swirling waters, swollen by the storm. It took more than an hour to bring him back to life. I sheltered him by spreading out my cloak to cover him. He did not see me at once. As soon as he opened his eyes he saw my father, who was putting away in his bag the instruments he had just been using. Then, with his unwounded arm, he did his best to pull a pistol from his trouser pocket, and I am certain that, had circumstances been more in his favour, he would have used it. But I knew that his powder was soaking wet and I said to him coldly: 'How do you feel now?' still holding my cloak over him. He raised his eyes to look at me and said: 'Who are you both?' Although he lay at full length in the mud, he had an air of great authority. 'I am a doctor,' my father told him,

131

'and I hope I have treated you well. Not like the man who shot you from behind. It was lucky for you that we had to come along this road at the time we did, and that we are not afraid of lightning. Another quarter of an hour and the torrent would have swept you away.'

"'I almost committed an unpardonable crime,' said the man. 'Have you a little alcohol?'

"'That is precisely what I am about to give you,' my father replied, unscrewing the stopper of his flask. The moment he had drunk it, the man rose to his feet and stood amazingly straight.

"'Could you manage to stay upright and walk as far as the horses that are tethered to a pine tree on the other side of the road?'

"'Certainly,' he said. In fact he needed no assistance.

"'Now,' said my father, 'here is the truth. It's a bad wound, especially in the back. You realise I have not probed it. It is essential that I should remove the bullet that is still there, but I live a league and a half away.'

"'I can walk.'

"'After a hundred yards the pain would be unbearable. Every step would jar your shoulder like a hammer blow. Believe me, you would not get far. It does not depend simply upon your will power. Do you feel up to riding a horse?'

"'Perfectly,' he replied, 'but I see there are only two.'

"'And how many do you want?' my father asked.

"'I will never agree,' said the man, 'to either of you walking.' In spite of the twilight and the mist in the rain-swept ravine, I clearly saw him smile. It was strange to see him forget his own needs and treat us with such punctilious courtesy. But it was so natural, so spontaneous, that my father simply said to him: 'Do not worry. My daughter will ride pillion behind me.'

"Then the man mounted unaided and settled himself in the saddle. He seemed to have a fancy not to touch the reins. True, we moved only at a walking pace. But between his thighs my mare, though she is terrified of thunder, stepped forward as serenely as a cat. We reached home without meeting anyone, for the storm had grown increasingly black and threatening and put out the street-lamps. That same evening, the two bullets were extracted. I say two, for the man had a hip wound that we had not seen. 'It is incredible,' my father said to me. 'Do you remember how well he sat his horse? He must be a veritable Chinaman!'

"Everything had seemed so strange to me, ever since the moment when, through the blinding rain, I had seen the man's legs floating in the torrent; I was so impressed by the haughty silence with which he endured pain that I asked, stupidly and with some disappointment, whether he was really a Chinaman.

"'My meaning was,' said my father, 'that he has a nobility, courage and strength of character that can come only from a very ancient mode of life. For the rest, my child, he is probably from somewhere hereabouts, but he has not said a word, and, by God, I am not the man to question him.'

"I asked whether he would recover. 'Very quickly,' said my father. 'I have never seen a more healthy body.' However he stayed in bed for a few days, in a little room on the second storey of our house. I was very curious to see him again.

"Our old servant used to take him his meals, but one day I took the tray from her and went up myself. The slatted shutters were closed, and the room was darkened still more by the foliage of a chestnut tree that covered the window. I did not see him as well as I could have wished, and he persistently refused to let me wait upon him. He made me go back down and send up Nathalie to cut his meat for him.

"After a week in our house he began to get up and walk about his room. I could tell from the sound that he used to go and sit by the window. I did not tell you, I think, that it was May. The weather was beautiful, and every evening I would go for a walk in the avenue of lime trees that leads up towards the old *hospice*. It is a local custom. There, I was with friends. We would wear our prettiest clothes and the young men came and looked at us. Sometimes in the shade we would play with hoops or join in a game of battledore. I am slim and nimble, and played well. They used to court us, in the rough and ready, rather coarse fashion that is the height of daring for lads in little country towns amid wild hills. The heart is of no importance, but money means a great deal. If I have told you that, from this point of view, they looked down upon my father, it will explain the boorishness of these yokels who would sometimes seize me round the middle, while we were playing, as though I were a goat. 'You are sure to get married,' my friends would say to me. 'How lucky you are to have such large eyes and to be so slender. Your clothes look lovely when you run fast, and you always looked intrigued. The boys think it is on their account. They feel flattered.' Heaven preserve me from ever having thought of them in that way, not even in my loneliest hours! Besides, my solitude was never unhappy. Quite the opposite. My father is the most wonderful man in the world for making solitude one continuous delight. Long before I could read he led me through Ariosto's forests and into those palaces of Madrid where Calderón opens secret doors. How often I felt like boxing Hamlet's ears with this little hand! I was sure that, in Ophelia's place, I should have found something better to do than drowning myself!

"I fell madly in love a hundred times. There were plenty of handsome men in my books, and I assure you that

Roland would not have gone mad if I had been with him. But in the avenue of lime trees there was no Roland, no Hamlet, no one at all. Do you know how one of my friends managed to find herself a husband? It was quite easy. She learned by heart the prices paid for calves at every cattle market for leagues around. She became a sort of barometer on the subject. She amazed a great red-haired fellow who was certainly the best catch in the whole neighbourhood. He weighed two hundred pounds and could not run – he was hopeless at rounders – but he was caught like a butter-fly in a hat by her practical knowledge of matters that were essential for a man in his profession. He was a cattle dealer at the port of Toulon, an agent for victualling ships of the navy – she gave us a whole list of his titles. And do you know what she valued most in her love affair? She whispered it in my ear behind her white veil when I kissed her in the vestry: 'And now, my poppet, we'll have children! Quickly! I do not want a single sou to slip through my fingers.'

"I do not like boys. If you want them, all you have to do is to surprise them, with your large eyes or your knowledge of the price of calves. But where is the man to surprise me?

"My father could and did. But, alas he was my father. I had to hide from him almost all the reasons for my tender-ness when I kissed him ardently upon his strange eyes and his pretty little prickly beard.

"One evening, then, while I was playing prisoners' base I noticed, leaning against the trunk of a lime tree, a sort of groom or postilion. He was still breathless from hard riding and bathed in sweat. His horse was licking his shoulder. When the game was over he came up to me and asked if I was the doctor's daughter. 'Tell me the way,' said he, 'and I will go and wait for you at your door. If anyone enquires what I said to you, reply that I asked you about the road to

Saint-Paul.' He did, in fact, take that road, but I had told him of a little side lane that led off it.

"Soon after, I reached home myself, but I had been thinking. I knew my father was gone to Artigues where one of his patients was having a baby, and things like that sometimes take a long time. He might be away all night. I found the groom's precautions disquieting. There was already enough mystery about the two wounds our guest had received. I was still more inclined to be suspicious when the groom asked after the wounded man. I made him some reply, while I casually slipped my hand into the drawer where my father kept his pistol, but at the moment when I pulled out the weapon our patient himself appeared and caught me in the act of threatening the groom, whose eyes bulged with surprise.

"'Thank you, Mademoiselle,' he said, laughing 'but this man is my servant. I was expecting him. In his bag he has brought me some fine linen and fresh clothes, in which I look forward to paying my respects to so much courage and so much charm!' And he kissed my hand, the one holding the pistol, which could not benefit from his kiss as fully as I could have wished.

"Whenever my father was away from home I used to take my meals alone. That night, there was a hint of magic in the air. The groom had gone, after bowing to me with considerable respect. Hardly had Nathalie come to serve my soup, when I heard the man come down from his room. The door of the dining room stood open, but a curtain hung before it. He stopped behind the curtain and said: 'Will you permit me, Mademoiselle?' Then he came in. He was like a prince. He was wearing closefitting trousers of very fine beige cloth, stretched over his calves and thighs by the straps under his insteps. His shirt was of soft silk, cut loosely, with billowing sleeves. A red silk scarf supported his arm on the side of his wounded shoulder. He came forward and said: 'Allow me to wait on you.' I was like a marble statue. Then he did a very difficult thing: he made the fantastic suggestion seem natural and serene. He smiled, and added: 'I knew you would not be upset.' And I did, in fact, take my meal, that evening, with perfect composure, served by him, as though I had been used to such service from the day I was born. I heard myself say to Nathalie in the most natural manner in the world: 'Make us some coffee, ma bonne.' He sat in the armchair facing me, and talked to me. It was the sort of conversation I had longed for of old, and knew so well. How many times had I talked to myself in the same strain! That gave me a surprising ease of manner. I was overwhelmed by the marvels he recounted. But I was so eager to hear them that not once did he see me out of breath or ill at ease. Step by step I kept pace with him as he explored those heights, while to myself I said: 'Since he is alive, since all this is true and possible, what else do I want from life? Can I ever find anyone else with his delicate perceptions, his appreciation of all that is noble?'

"No one knew that this man was in our house. Nathalie was loyal to me, body and soul. One evening he said: 'Can you keep me here until my wound is sufficiently healed not to affect my arm movements?' 'Two months will be enough for that,' said my father, 'but in a fortnight's time you ought to exercise your arm and your body. Nothing would be better for you than riding. Have you any reasons for staying shut up indoors?' 'None whatever,' the man replied, 'if you will allow Mademoiselle to come riding with me.'

"The groom came back, bringing a horse, the finest I had ever seen. Nor had I ever known anything lovelier than that month of August. One afternoon we rode out together for the first time. He took me straight to the place where we had found him. 'No traces can still have remained,' he said, 'but I imagine my horse came down to the river to drink. I was unconscious and must have fallen, for the place where I was attacked was further away. Let us look, in case there may still be hoofprints.' We pulled aside the rushes and marsh-samphire, and at last we found the print of four iron shoes. In my mind's eye I could see the horse with his empty saddle. He must have stood there a moment, looking at his fallen rider and waiting for a sign, an order that never came. Then he started off alone over the hill, terrified, perhaps, by a dazzling flash of lightning, leaving in my path the man I was fated to meet.

"'Let us go up to the high ground,' he said. He rode on ahead, schooling his horse to a gentle gallop that my mare could follow comfortably. He sat his mount admirably. He was thin and supple, wholly made up of muscles accustomed to winning the finest things of life. The line of his broad shoulders, in spite of his wound, lay as straight and true as the arm of a balance that has settled into rest. We rode for more than a league before we saw, at ten paces from the road, a thick plantation of juniper trees. 'That is where they were,' he said. 'Come.' We dismounted, and leading our horses by their bridles, went into the covert. I should tell you that all this took place in the lonely woods of Vacon, on the deserted stretch of road leading from Rians to Saint-Maximin through the mountains of Séouves. 'Let us tether our horses,' he suggested. 'Unless I am much mistaken, I am going to show you something that will raise your spirits.' The undergrowth was very thick, and he held the branches aside for me to pass. As we came to the junipers he stopped and turned towards me. 'I imagine,' said he, 'you would not like it if anyone could snap at me without my biting them?'

"In the midst of those rough bushes I felt, I do assure

you, as warm and sheltered as I do at this moment, wrapped in your capes in this armchair. 'I like you to be as you are,' I replied.

"'Then look,' said he. 'That is where they are,' and he stood aside.

"At first I could see nothing but a brown mass, but I was fascinated and drew closer. There, scattered by bees and foxes, lay the bodies of two men who had been three months dead.

"'I aimed at the flashes of their guns,' he said. 'It would have been surprising if my bullets had gone wide.'

"'I am very glad they hit their target,' I replied.

"'It was most humiliating for me that you might have taken me for the sort of man who can be shot at without retaliating.'

"'I have never thought that,' I answered, looking him straight in the face.

"He turned his eyes away a little, as though embarrassed by my certainty. 'On that night,' he went on, 'there had already been a sort of crime committed on the high-road from Saint-Maximin to Aix. The coach from Nice had been robbed of a treasure chest of public funds. I had been warned and was on the alert. These fellows always like to scatter into the woods, once the attack is over. Besides look here.' He turned over the debris with the toe of his boot and uncovered two felt hats with the skulls still in them.

"Have I made you fully understand that this man had never touched me, not even with the tips of his fingers, except once, when he kissed my hand? Yet he had made me enter his own magnificent domain. So now it was absolutely imperative that I should make him understand me, not as I seem to be, but as I am, and let him know that anything of his would be loved and respected. It was very important that I should do it at once and unmistakably; it was so easy for him to withdraw himself, even with his eyes. I asked him for his pistol. He handed it to me at once, quite unconcerned. I am not very skilled, but I put so much of my soul into it that my first shot smashed one of those dirty little skulls to powder.

"'Good,' he said. 'That means more to me than you can imagine, Mademoiselle. Allow me to reload that weapon. Nothing would give me more pleasure than to hear you shoot again.' And I gladly fired a second time at the remains of the men he had laid low in defence of his own life."

"That is the man you should have married," said the Marquise. She had stopped weeping, but her breath came noisily.

"Have you noticed," said the young woman, "that I have not yet said anything about his age? I admired his firm, lean body. He was tireless on horseback. He taught me to shoot with a pistol and I've become very good at it. As for him, his eye was keen, his wrist infallible. Once he had reached a decision he was never troubled by remorse; his characteristic quality was a blend of action and speed. Often he began his sentences with: 'Allow me,' or 'Will you permit me?' but every time it was to exert his will. 'Allow me,' he said one evening, 'to accompany you to that avenue of limes where you never go now, and where, I believe, games are played.'

"I realised that he was impelled to ask me this by the same sort of necessity that had made me fire on the relics of his dead enemies. You can imagine my joy. He played with us, light and quick as the boys, but he astonished me. I was filled with admiration, for, in the speed of the game, he was carrying the additional burden of his long rides on horseback and hampered by his courtesy, his nobility. So, when everything was settled and my father said to me:

'He is sixty-eight years old.' 'What does he know of age?'
I replied."

"What? What?" cried the Marquise. She seemed
thunderstruck. "You little deceiver!" she said to her tenderly. "How well you protect yourself! And only twenty!
Let me look at those innocent eyes of yours! But it is
impossible to recognise my brother in your story! It cannot
be Laurent! Yet it is, down to a T! What was he doing in
that part of the country, which must, I should think, be
inhabited by all the tigresses of Hyrcania, if you are only a
little girl, as your face suggests and as I believe?"

She asked endless questions, insisted on her rehearsing
every detail of the fortunate chance that led them to
find him. "His legs were floating, did you say?" She could
not imagine it. "Floating!" she repeated, with a pout of
her thick lips. "You will not get out of it any longer, with
all your pretty ways. I am old enough to know what
talking really means. All that is a charming rigmarole, but
you have not answered my question. Are you happy? How
long is it since you were married? Five months? Good!
That simply proves that you are stubborn. As I knew
from your forehead, anyway. Now listen carefully to what
I tell you. One cannot live on reputation . . . not even
when that reputation is justified. Just what that means, I
will not explain to you for all the gold in the world.
I no longer know whether I ought to answer the questions
in your great eyes, or talk to the Amazon in you. And yet,
it's a fawn you look like. I saw it at once. In any case, I am
being foolish. You may be a fawn or a little panther, but
neither fawns nor panthers have any common sense. Don't
listen to what I'm saying. You know nothing about it.
Go and open the window! I'm stifling! No! Don't move!
You would catch cold!"

They spent all the rest of the night unweariedly telling

each other, over and over again, what they had said already. "But you understand nothing of love, my angel," the Marquise declared, and began to explain it to her at great length. In the end, as the dawn was whitening the windows, the girl fell peacefully asleep in her armchair.

"To sleep is to be satisfied," sighed the Marquise, freed from the scrutiny of those great eyes.

9

ONE DAY IN EARLY December Angelo returned to
Marseilles and went to see the fat woman, Paula. She had a
packet for him. It contained first a note from the Genoese
sailor, a pitiful little scrawl in his own dialect: "The Duchess
has been so kind as to consider me the best man to be your
messenger and your servant. I am very proud of that, for we
have managed to shut the mouths of all those who spoke
ill of your lordship. In all the cafés of Genoa, and all the
inns of the Turin road, people are now saying that you are
the man to pull the ears of the Pope and deliver Rome into
our hands. The Duchess has taken my mother and my
youngest brother under her protection. So I am free to tell
the world what I think, and I took a hand in a little disci-
plinary action against those two misbegotten green squirts
who made you go away. It will keep them in bed for the
next six months. I am just starting on a voyage to Algiers,
and if you have no orders for me in two months' time I will
make another trip to Barcelona. I have explained everything
very clearly to the fat woman. She is like me, entirely at
your service."

Above all she was completely terrified. She begged
Angelo not to go away without leaving a word or two to
testify, beyond any possible doubt, that she had faithfully
carried out her instructions. "If they are talking about me
like that," Angelo thought to himself, "and saying I ought
to pull the Pope's ears, I had better be very careful about
writing or signing anything. Not to mention any friends
the 'misbegotten squirts' may have." The fat woman, misunderstanding the reason behind Angelo's hesitation, burst
into tears and sobbed: "I assure you that I did just as Beppo

told me. It is more than three weeks ago that I unpicked the stitching of my palliasse without a light, and hid your packet in the straw. I was constantly reminded of it whenever I lay down, for it was hard. It has made a purple bruise on my back that I will show you if you like. Not only did I keep my door locked, but two or three times every day I would go up to make sure your packet was still there. And I give you my word I told absolutely nothing to the man who came trying to winkle anything he could out of me."

For too long, Angelo had been bored, and her last homely phrase gave him a quiver of delight. "What sort of a man was he?" he asked.

"He looked like a mason," the woman told him.

"A trick by my friend who appoints foremen," thought Angelo. "But how did he know I had any dealings with this woman? Dear land of mine!" He felt a surge of joy at coming again into touch with this systematic spying and counter-spying. "Don't worry," he said to the woman, "and do as you are told," he added, so gravely that she began to sob again. "Here is something for you to show Beppo, and he will be very nice to you. Give me one of those large sheets of grey paper you use to make a cornet when you sell your mussels." He dipped his fingers in some red wine and printed a line from Dante: *Di sotto al capo mio son li altri tratti*, "Beneath my head the other [Popes] are dragged." "And now, take me to your room and see that I am not disturbed."

He opened the packet and found a letter from his mother. Angelo read it through several times. He could not have enough of this breath of air from Turin. At last, he called the fat woman and she let him out by a door giving on to a street in the old quarter.

When he arrived back in Aix he found Mme Hortense

in a fine state. "Rosette has been three times," she told him. "You are wanted at the Vicar-General's."

On that same day, towards six o'clock in the morning, the Vicar-General had had a surprise. He had not yet put on his cassock, and in riding breeches and shirtsleeves he was shaving in front of a little glass lit by a bright reflector-lamp, when there came a knock on his door. Without being violent, the blows were very sharp. "That's the metal end of a riding whip," said he to himself. The knocks came again. "A silver one," he added as he went towards the door, casting a furtive glance around the room to make sure all was in order. Then he drew the bolts and opened the door. It was the Marquis of Théus.

"Have I surprised you?" he asked.

"In the middle of shaving, yes. Come in."

The Marquis was in riding dress, and smelt slightly of sweat and wet cloth. "Who is this boy you're wanting me to trip over?" he asked curtly.

"I do not concern myself with boys, nor with tripping you," said the Vicar-General. "Come in so I can shut the door. It's cold enough to freeze a duck." He went across to lift the lid of a little saucepan heating on a tripod in the embers of the fireplace. "Will you have some coffee?"

"I have had more coffee than I want," replied the Marquis. "All I need this morning is a few clear explanations."

"I think I can provide you with them," said the Vicar-General, carefully lathering his chin.

"I have just come from the Archbishop's," said the Marquis.

"How is his gout?" asked the Vicar.

"Much improved."

"Which is? The gout or the Archbishop?"

"They make a perfect pair."

145

"Then I understand your meaning," said the Vicar-General.

"You do not seem to understand that I work at night," said the Marquis. "Nothing, I confess, is more touching than your little bachelor establishments, the remedies on the Archbishop's bedside table, and, here, the pan of coffee among the embers. The heavens would not fall if that fellow over there employed a *valet-de-chambre*, and you, a servant of some sort here. But you have your own weapons and I do not question them. Do not question mine."

"I am well aware of the whole position," the Vicar-General replied. "You must recognise that I have not left you unaware of the fact that I approve neither your methods of combat nor your plan of campaign."

"We are not obliged to be in agreement," said the Marquis.

"Not obliged, certainly not. But everything would go much better if we were."

"I do not see in what respect things would go better," the Marquis retorted. "Anyhow, was I chosen by the council? I'll answer for that."

"So was I," said the Vicar-General.

"It was understood that nothing but results would count. It is two years since I took command. I am solely responsible for creating the organisation that, in a year and a half, has brought you one million, seven hundred thousand francs. A million the first year, and seven hundred thousand in the last six months . . . Without any risks . . . for you, at least, since they are all on my own head. Again, this very night, I have brought in a hundred and fifty thousand crowns."

"This past night?" exclaimed the Vicar-General. "What part of the country were you working in? Haven't they planned a system of mounted escorts? The Chief of Police was talking to me, under the seal of secrecy, about a network of mobile patrols and I don't know how many control points. It would, of course, be quite easy to find out for you exactly where they are, for all the good it would do you."

"Do not concern yourself with what the police get up to," the Marquis cut in, "nor the places where I work, nor with my ways of working. Count the millions, that is all I ask of you. You cannot pretend that yours is a very exacting role. I have always agreed that the clergy have particular gifts for managing fortunes. Manage the one I bring you. You are in your right place, and I am in mine. But when I arrive with the intention of taking off my riding boots for five minutes I should be glad not to have to argue for hours over subtle points of intrigue with a prelate who uses his gout as I do my pistols."

"For hours?" said the Vicar-General. "How thoughtless of him! You have my deepest sympathy. Do take off your boots here in perfect safety, dear friend. I will find a pair of slippers to lend you."

"For three months, this summer, I have been keeping your Syrian bishop, who made no secret of the fact that he was there to watch me," the Marquis went on. "I have brought him back to you. Send him off to pass the plate round under the cedars of Lebanon. That's all he is fit for. Take it from me, if ever he finds a gold piece in his collection he will fall on his knees in the dust. He is not made for enterprises that demand a cool head. He very nearly landed me in the soup over the affair at Peyrolles. And now it's a young man you're on about."

"Do not lay all the sins of Israel to my charge," said the Vicar-General, powdering his cheeks. "I have told you nothing, myself."

"Who will you manage to convince," the Marquis replied coldly, "that His Lordship has any ideas of his own?"

"No one, if I'm any judge of current opinion," the Vicar-General replied. "But you saw for yourself that he can use gout with remarkable skill. Admit that his malady gives him a certain force of character. I have no need to put forward suggestions at such times."

"And if you had done so after all, simply out of habit, he would have been delighted, I imagine, to find an idea; all ready to his hand, as usual. That is what I thought, at a guess."

"And that's where you're wrong. In your turn, who would you manage to convince that your nightly enterprises are all a matter of chance? They are too perfectly organised to be other than thoroughly well thought out. Use the same argument in this case. Although, as I realise, the thing borders on the miraculous, His Lordship does, now and then, have an idea of his own. And you may well believe," he went on with a laugh, "that I am the first to regret it. But I sense that you are not to be persuaded," he added, opening a little cupboard in the wall and taking out two cups.

"I have already played a game of wits with the Archbishop," remarked the Marquis in a casual tone. "I was hoping that here we should do each other the mutual honour of a little plain speaking."

"You mentioned a young man," said the Vicar-General as he arranged the cups on the table. "If it is the young man I think, you know him. You not only know him, you have already chosen him."

"I chose him? What for?"

"To carry out a mission that called for nothing more than simplicity of mind, a considerable absence of guile. That will tell you what a rare bird he is."

"I do not know any simpletons."

"Now is your chance to meet one, the like of which we

148

shall never see again," said the Vicar-General, "especially if our schemes are successful. Take advantage of it. But, I repeat, you have already done so."

"I do not recall ever having taken advantage of a simpleton."

"He does not lack nobility, as well I know," the Vicar-General replied, pouring coffee into the cups. "Carry your mind back a few months, will you? Actually, to that affair at Peyrolles you specifically mentioned just now. Do you recall how worried I was about the success of that project, which seemed to me to start off badly? So much so, that I ventured to criticise your methods and propose a radical change at the secret council."

"All you did was to delay my action for an hour," said the Marquis.

"And you sent to advise me of your success by the hand of a young man wearing white corduroy."

"Is that the man we are talking of?"

"I imagine so."

"I decidedly prefer to play this game with you, instead of with the Archbishop," said the Marquis, picking up his cup of coffee. "You know me as well as if you had made me. Your little tricks are always directed at some idiosyncrasy of mine. It is evident that here we have a skilful economy in the use of resources, a point that appeals to me. I chance to avail myself of the services of a certain youth. He is the very one you send back to me. I cannot deny myself the pleasure of joining in your game – and you knew I couldn't."

"It is a pleasure to talk to a man of spirit," commented the Vicar-General.

"I quite agree," returned the Marquis. "No one ever appeals in vain to my taste for things that are perfect, and difficult. I will take the boy."

"I'll wager that His Lordship resorted to a thousand tiny falsehoods in attempting to persuade you," the Vicar-General remarked.

"Of course, he lacks your sense of what is fitting," replied the Marquis. "Then, too, I refuse to argue with him. What I refuse, as a matter of fact, is not so much whatever he proposes, as any combat worth the name. But he hasn't even the cunning to take that fact into account, and to realise that in the long run he would get what he wants because of my sheer distaste for an argument with him. I shall end by saying yes. You well know that I am too much of a gambler not to accept a game when it is offered me. But without pleasure. While with you, I enjoy it."

"Yes," said the Vicar-General. "In our chess-game certain moves along the diagonal were denied to me. You've presented me with a bishop – maybe a fool – so why shouldn't I make a move with him?"

"Then it would rest with me to take him again," the Marquis answered. "With a bishop and a couple of knights I can perfectly well put you in check."

"This youth will give you a great deal of pleasure," said the Vicar-General. "He is now very well dressed, an expert at fencing and with the sabre, and he puts so much richness of feeling into intrigue that, for anyone who knows the signs, he is a sight to see."

As soon as the Marquis had left, the Vicar-General went into Rosette's room. "Don't think you can lie in bed all morning," said he, seating himself in a white satin armchair. "Get up and run over to your mother's. I want the little colonel."

Angelo did not arrive at the Vicar-General's house until after dark. "You cannot imagine how much my life is centred on you," the churchman told him. "I have sent three times to find you, and now I was beginning to despair. What did you go to do in Marseilles? It is only my tender care for you that prompts the question."

"Shall I tell him about my mother?" Angelo debated. "Bah! Why not? A fine bit of farce, and she would enjoy it, to tell the truth to a man who has me watched, and yet overlooked the fact that I can always go and lose myself among the three hundred thousand inhabitants of a port less than twenty leagues away. But not a word about the sailor. He would be quite capable of having him arrested." He said aloud: "I am more deeply touched than I can say. I had written to my mother."

"By post?" exclaimed the Vicar-General.

"Why not?" replied Angelo. "I have nothing to hide. Only I took the precaution of asking her to reply to me at Marseilles, at the *poste restante*, the usual custom in such a port. A letter coming from Piedmont would have attracted attention in Aix. That is what I went to look for."

"I admire you," said the Vicar-General. "You really do know how to steer clear of trouble every time. Those were extremely wise precautions. And . . . have you had the reply?"

"No," Angelo replied. "It was only a month ago that I wrote. I was too eager. Otherwise I should have reckoned more accurately how long it would take for a reply to arrive. Especially at this time of the year, when boats can so easily be delayed by bad weather. What I shall have to do is to go back there again a few days before Christmas."

"That will, perhaps, be difficult," the Vicar-General remarked, "for I have a service to ask of you. It will, moreover, be a very pleasant task, but you will need to leave Aix tomorrow."

"Say nothing," Angelo warned himself. "Perhaps there is something behind all this that my mother will find most entertaining."

"Do you remember the chateau of La Vallette?" continued the Vicar, after trying to assess Angelo's short silence.

"Extremely well."

"The suggestion is that you should spend some time there. The Marquis himself invites you."

"For long?"

"That will depend. Have you any objection to a long stay?"

"Not the least in the world. I thought it a most picturesque place with its luxuriant foliage and the solitude of the park. There was a pool I particularly liked."

"True," added the Vicar-General, "the winter must be somewhat depressing there."

"Depression does not worry me," said Angelo.

"So I have noticed, as you may imagine," the Vicar-General answered with a smile.

"And what am I going to do at La Vallette?"

"Conduct yourself like an ordinary guest, that's all. Were you thinking I might have something else in mind?"

"You spoke of a service I was to do for you."

"You do not love me," sighed the Vicar. "Otherwise you would understand my loving care for you. I see you wasting your generous nature upon people of no account. You live in a cheerless street. In spite of all the efforts of a heart that deserves something better, the only friends you have are a few common swordsmen. If we refer to them as friends, it is because this provincial town, which is steeped in mud one moment and dust the next, has nothing better to offer. Even your love affairs . . . I have dreamed of a more brilliant setting for your personality. Not the world of fashion, with its sordid temptations, which in the end has the same poverty, if somewhat gilded, but in an atmosphere where nobility reaches its most sublime purity. Did you not tell me of your emotion at the very sight of the façade of that chateau at La Vallette? I wanted to give you the companionship of minds that inspired the creation of these noble works. You, too, have a certain magnificence, my boy. On the one hand, I can fully appreciate your intense interest in the sight and sounds of winter parklands swept by the north winds, but, on the other, I profoundly distrust the petty, mechanical way of life that can, by pinpricks, bleed your spirit dry when it is seething with heroic blood. We, the Marquis and I, have a certain common interest in a high endeavour that must remain unknown to you. But it is men of this quality that should be your companions, to prepare you for a brilliant destiny. There, my son, is the service I ask of you. Let me help you to become what you should be. I shall never ask any other service of you. Of that, you may be sure."

Angelo was acutely embarrassed. "What sincerity in his eyes!" he was saying to himself. "Everything he says is straight from the heart. He is the most saintly man I have ever met. And would you deceive such a man? No! You shall not sink to such ingratitude . . . I lied to you just now," he said, and went on to relate his visit to Marseilles just as it happened. He spoke of the Genoese sailor, drew his mother's letter from his pocketbook and gave it to the Vicar-General to read.

"Do not paint yourself blacker than you are," said he magnanimously. "You had every right to conceal something from me, and when it was simply a message from a mother to a son, I do not see what you can be accused of. Let us admit there was no need for you to invent your story of tempests and the *poste restante*, but the world will not come to an end if we call it merely an indiscretion of the imagination." Nevertheless, he had put on his spectacles and read the Duchess' letter with close attention. "Usually, one assumes," said he, giving the letter back to Angelo, "that children are worthy of their parents; allow me to tell you in this case that your mother is worthy of you. What enthusiasm! What wisdom! What is she like? Blonde or brunette?"

"Blonde," replied Angelo. "She is from the north of Piedmont."

"I love these women," the Vicar-General observed, "who possess a deep insight into human feelings and still allow themselves to be swayed by emotion, preferring to run the risk of being imposed on, rather than letting their generous impulses shrivel and die. Beyond question, the greatest happiness we can know on this earth is to stay young. Nothing can take the place of enthusiasm, a zest for life. Between the man who knows, but holds back, and one who does not know, yet wholeheartedly gives of his best, I always try my utmost to be the latter. I do not always succeed – hardly ever, perhaps I should say – save in what concerns you. I am carried away by those rare qualities I see in you. You are my youth. If I needed to give a reason for my affection, that is what I should have to say. I speak to you as your mother does. I, too, hope that God will befriend you, and pray that He will lead your steps into the wilderness of love. Your mother knew how to find the right word! I well understand that sublime souls may weary of the use they seem obliged to make of the divine creation. I understand it because God, in His infinite goodness, understood it first, and created souls for whom the ordinary passing show, the commonplace things of life, could never suffice. So He, in His perfect understanding has vouchsafed a special boon to men of your quality, permitting them to approach love through a sort of wilderness, a boundless solitude where you are dazzled by the blazing heavens and can conjure up your mirages and live in a world of your own creation. But I'm getting carried away into preaching a little homily to no purpose. Let us speak of earthly things. You must set out in the morning at the earliest possible moment. The Marquis is expecting you tomorrow night."

Angelo went home bewildered and trembling with excitement. He found it strange that he had managed to live in Aix for so many tedious months. "He is right," he thought to himself. "What have I done up to now? Nothing except swordplay and a little artificial love-making much against my inclination, for my heart was never in it. Everything here is mean and paltry. But for this fine man, I should probably soon have reached the stage of having my own pipe-rack in the café *Deux Garçons*, and getting pot-bellied in spite of all the exercise I take. I had no fancy for becoming a foreman among those navvies, yet that was the only place where I could have put a little heart into what I was doing."

Before packing his luggage, he locked his door and put out his candles. It was a long time since he had opened the little leather pouch where he kept the perfumed kerchief. The night was very dark, with driving rain blown by a wind strong enough to rattle the windows. Yet he found the thongs of the sachet and indulged himself by savouring the lovely fragrance for several lingering moments of delight.

He rose before dawn and ran to the coaching stables to hire a cabriolet. "Fifteen leagues in weather like this is no joke, sir," the head stableman told him. "Especially on the roads of Var. I know that part of the country like the back of my hand. You'll have to ford a hundred gullies or more, and at this time of the year, with the rain we've had the last three days, they'll be worse than the Durance. I certainly cannot see a cabriolet fitting into that sort of picture. I know your reason for wanting one: you like to travel fast. You young fellows are all the same. In your place I would take a brougham with two good horses. In any case, since you are not coming back, you must have a driver. The horses and the man I will give you are capable of getting you over any bad patches, and the axle is high enough to clear all the fords. The journey will take you three hours longer, but haven't you ever lost more time than that for reasons far less sound? You can see for yourself, this is no weather for fancy travelling."

The wind and rain had indeed redoubled during the night and were battering the old elms of the boulevard so roughly that a great bough was torn off and fell with a loud noise, scraping the front of the house. "Your cabriolet would be a fine lot of good if accidents like that were to happen to you in the woods of Var. Believe me, sir, the brougham is not so stylish (you see, I know all your reasons), but more reliable." Finally Angelo gave in, on condition that the carriage should be at his door within an hour to load up his luggage.

Mme Hortense gave the impression of having spent the whole night before her dressing-table mirror. In spite of the very early hour – the day had not yet dawned, though there was just enough light to show that the sky was alarmingly black – her hair was beautifully dressed, and she was powdered and perfumed, her little collar of white lace faultlessly starched. She gave every sign of being most distressed, though she did not forget to raise the lid of her coffee-pot now and then, so that her coffee should not boil. "I shall miss you sadly," she told him. "It is enough to break my heart to see you taking away your things. I had grown used to you. For the first time in years I felt esteem, and perhaps something more, for someone living under my roof. I will keep your rooms just as they are. I shall put fresh flowers in them twice a week, and clean sheets in the bed. Remember the little garden door, also that I am deaf, dumb and blind.

I shall take great pleasure in keeping for you a secret, downy nest." There was something in her expression as she spoke that did not please Angelo. Still, as he thanked her, he ventured on the familiarity of patting her shoulder.

The coachman was no more than half an hour late. Before picking up the luggage he looked carefully around. "I have heard a great deal about you, sir," he said, "and know you are brave. That is why I agreed to drive you. But where are your pistols, or at the very least, your sword? The country we have to go through is not particularly Catholic. Travellers are often held up there."

"Don't worry," said Angelo. He was beginning to enjoy the roaring of the wind, and the coachman's anxiety conjured up enchanting possibilities. "How did I manage to endure being shut up so long in that priest's cell?" he wondered. Joyfully he breathed in the freezing dampness of the dawn.

"That's good enough for me," replied the driver. "With a man like you I would go to the ends of the earth. But how shall I manage on the way back?"

"You'll manage very well," Angelo assured him, "with the two crowns I will give you as your tip."

"Now you're talking," exclaimed the man. "Come on. Off we go."

"Remember that here you have a home and discreet friends," Mme Hortense repeated with a hideous smile as the carriage rattled away.

Angelo arrived at La Vallette at ten o'clock in the evening after a very dull journey with nothing exceptional about it, apart from the time it took. Even the wind and rain lost their violence after daybreak and settled down into an ordinary wet winter's day. The gullies that the head ostler had talked about turned out to be merely muddy brooks too shallow to reach the horses' knees. "That was a fine trick to play on me," Angelo told the driver. "I could perfectly well have forded those in a cabriolet." "The fact is," said the man, "that no one has hired the brougham for a long time, and Pierrot made the best of his opportunity. He gets a bonus on the number of wheels, and I myself, over and above the two crowns you promised me, have a better chance to make a bit on the side with oats for two horses. Don't look down your nose at that, sir. We all have a living to make."

As they were crossing the hills that rolled away before them like waves, the driver pointed out to Angelo a few huge juniper trees rearing their heads high above the scrub. "What I told you about brigands," said he, "is only too true. They post their sentinels under those trees, as a rule. There's nothing to stop them carrying out their trade in broad daylight." The countryside was, in very truth, utterly deserted as far as the eye could see. "And what could we do if they were to attack us?"

"Fight them," said Angelo. "Speak for yourself," the man retorted. "I happen to be the father of a family. The two crowns you promised me are still in your pocket."

"And there they will stay, unless you whip up your horses. They're fast asleep."

"Hold on, sir. Look over there, under that juniper. If that isn't a man on horseback, my name isn't . . . Speak of a wolf, and . . . Halt! And pull out your guns."

"Don't you try to make me take a brougham for a cabriolet again. Keep moving. It's a horseman but that's no reason for deciding he's a brigand."

Time after time as they travelled on, they caught sight of lonely riders who, in point of fact, did look like sentinels stationed under tall junipers. The last one, whom they passed as dusk was falling, was posted at the roadside. He looked an ugly customer, but made no attempt to obstruct them. He satisfied himself by following them for half a mile or so, a hundred yards behind, then he took a track leading off to the side, where they saw him trotting before he disappeared. The night closed in. Some long time later, the chateau of La Vallette, its great windows blazing with light, shone out from the high ground ahead, but they still had to wind their way through the thickets covering the plateau and its escarpment before they reached it.

"I had the state rooms lighted," said the Marquis, "so that, even from a distance, we should show you a sort of golden welcome. Alas, they are empty tonight: my sister has left us and the Marquise could not stay awake any longer. She is a child. She was falling asleep against the arm of her chair, so I told her: 'Go to bed. You will see him tomorrow. He is an excellent young man and will gladly excuse you.' Forgive my informal dress." He was wearing leather breeches, riding boots and a doeskin tunic. "Forgive me, too, for having asked your pardon in this bourgeois fashion. I remembered you as a man with the look of a stag. You still have the air of a denizen of the forest, proud and full of dreams. Since that look is in your eyes it is right that I should appear before you, not in starched linen and the fine cloth of Elbeuf, but as the king of the hills that I am."

"I myself am in travelling dress," Angelo replied, "and I thank heaven that Madame la Marquise was so sleepy. I should have been most upset if she had met me in my present state." To himself he was thinking with astonishment: "This is all on a very different note from our first encounter."

"You have no idea," the Marquis continued, "how fascinated my wife, I myself and all our household can be by the mud or dust of the highroad, and that bowed-forward look all long-distance travellers have in the curves of their spine until they are fully rested. I think there should be semi-circular coffins made for dead travellers. But no one can say you have come any great distance to get here from Aix. That is not what I mean, in your case. I am speaking of that long period of development, begun many years, perhaps, before your birth, that created the lines of your body just as, beyond all question, the shape of a horse's head was moulded by the wind in the course of countless years of evolution from prehistoric times."

The Marquis informed Angelo that his supper would shortly be served, and while waiting they paced up and down together on the carpets of the great salons.

"One thing that gives me a great advantage over many people," the Marquis observed, "and especially over men of the calculating type – you understand what I mean? Those who look to the future and plan and organise everything, surrounding themselves with every safeguard their intelligence can devise, like a fortification – is that I am a man of the open road. In you I recognise the same zestful impetuosity. We gain our ends in spite of everything, as waves do. We do not batter our way through obstacles, we circumvent them. We are centrifugal, like the ripples made by a pebble tossed into a pond. That's what I mean when I call myself a freelance, a man of the open road. There is such a thing as a bandit of the open road, a highwayman. Why not an honest highwayman? The only difficulty is that the term is customarily linked with 'a bandit', rather than with 'an honest man', and it is very hard to break a custom. Ah, well! We must put up with whatever people call us because of our love for the great outdoors and huge enterprises."

Supper was announced and they went into the dining room where a place was laid for one, at the head of an immense table fully set out with damask and crystal. As Angelo showed some embarrassment at all this magnificence arranged in his honour, the Marquis, taking his arm to conduct him to his seat, remarked: "Even if it were not for your rank, and the fact that men such as you are rare, there would still be a special respect due to you as a friend of that kindly man who fulfils the duties of Vicar-General to the Archbishop. The latter too, has warmly recommended you. I have no intention of keeping you under a bushel. All I have told you since your arrival shows very clearly that I mean you to enter fully into the life of our hill country, where there are splendours far more worthy of your admiration than this poor little show of luxury. Here we have no town life, no gay social occasions. We alternate between silence and tumult. So that you may savour the former, I have had furnished for you the little pavilion where you spent the night when I first had the honour of entertaining you.

"I do not want to weary you by the necessity of being our guest every day. There, you can be alone whenever you wish. The silences we have here are the most marvellous imaginable. I mean, quite literally, that they are full of marvels. A man is not always disposed to tell even his nearest and dearest all the intimate thoughts inspired in him by the wind that holds a forecast of snow, or the silent passing of a flock of wild geese against a patch of green sky. As for the tumults, all I can tell you about them is that they will be to your taste, and if I stress that point, you can believe me. Try some of this cold boar's head, but save your appetite for a dish of thrushes my chef has prepared specially for you. One might call them the game of this particular locality. Drink some of this wine from the Var. A friend of my father-in-law makes it expressly for my wife, and she herself decanted it for you at six o'clock this evening, when we knew you would be late in arriving."

Angelo had too keen a sense of the niceties of social behaviour to respond with anything other than banal courtesies, but his thoughts were overflowing with visions and extravagant phrases. "But," he said to himself, "nothing I want to say can be said in French. I should have to lapse into the dialect of Cuneo, where Theresa used to take me on holiday in the summer when I was seven years old. I saw wild geese there long ago." At last, blaming himself and in terror of appearing stupid or niggardly in his response, he managed to say: "I was a stranger even in my native land, save in my mother's palace, and in Aix I lived in a happy-go-lucky fashion that would soon have reduced me to despair and then to a pipe-rack in a café. Scarcely had I arrived here when you promised me happiness, and the wind that sweeps across your park assures me that the reality will exceed your promise. Shall I ever be able to offer you a service in recompense?"

"Let us understand each other on that point," the Marquis replied roundly. "I am quite grown up enough to tell you so without any reluctance, if I should need you."

Midnight sounded on a great clock, and lanterns were lit to conduct the traveller and his luggage to the pavilion. As he passed through the broad, icy corridor, Angelo shivered and felt the leather sachet rubbing against his skin. "It was here," he said to himself, "that I first grew aware of that lovely fragrance."

10

ANGELO WAS PROFOUNDLY MOVED to find himself
once again in the pavilion room. The little writing desk and
bookcase had been replaced by a large table in the style of
Henri II and some very comfortable armchairs. He walked
up and down for several minutes before recovering his
equanimity. There was no longer any trace of perfume. "It
was here," he reminded himself, "that I learned to choose,
and to insist on quality above all else. When I left, I had
doubtless vowed to live in solitude." Instantly his heart
conjured up a vision of heroic self-denial, and he gloried
in imagining a whole melancholy future for himself. Not
for anything in the world would he have wished for
such physical satisfaction as he had sometimes known with
Mme Clèves.

Two servants were on duty in the pavilion, where
everything, even a small kitchen, had been arranged for
his convenience, but before his little bachelor establishment
began to function Angelo was invited to the chateau. He
met the young Marquise and particularly noticed her magnificent black hair, but did not care for her great green eyes
that seemed to him cold and unwavering when her attention was captured. Her pallor and her elaborately formal
evening gown made her seem much older than her years.
Towards the end of the meal, just as she had made a startling comment or two about a certain valley lost in the
woods, he noticed how wide and flexible her mouth was.
"Her whole face could be held in my hands," he thought.
"She is like a little *fer de lance*."

He noticed no difference of age between the Marquis
and herself. The Marquis amazed him. Often he wore a

short pelisse made of sheepskin belted at the waist, which emphasised his height and his broad shoulders. On horse-back his movements were so supple that Angelo went to the window whenever he heard him galloping across the turf of the park, on his way back from the glen that the Marquise had mentioned so intriguingly, where there was a great sheepfold with twenty shepherds that Angelo was always promising himself to go and see. The Marquis would cross the immense stretch of greensward outside the pavilion windows at a slow *haute-école* canter, and the high-stepping deliberate action of his horse, transferred to the Marquis' body through his riding boots, made his torso quiver like a highly-tempered steel blade, most fascinating to watch. Angelo, who knew all the ways a man can come to terms with a horse, glowed with admiration for a rider who could create such perfectly co-ordinated movement.

"If you would like a sheepskin tunic like mine," said the Marquis, "that will be easy. The material and the artist are both at hand. There are fleeces already tanned and prepared at the farm, and my wife is very clever at making a paper pattern from which the village saddler cuts them out and sews them up. Get her to take your measurements. The winter is not over, and in any case our spring is very often worse than winter."

Angelo presented himself before the Marquise. "I have some very good blue tissue ready for you," she told him. "I am quite alone. Laurent has gone to the valley where the sheepfolds are. Come over by the fire and take off your coat. It's a lovely coat, but much too fine to wear here. Besides, there is a certain atmosphere about the *maquis* in winter, and you must attune yourself to it if you are to feel completely at ease. Are you like me? I attach a great importance to being in accord with one's surroundings, and that sort of harmony must always begin with externals. These sheepskin tunics are my own idea. You will see. As soon as you put one on you will understand this country much better. Your stomach is a little flatter than Laurent's. One centimetre. Your shoulders? Ah! Three centimetres wider. I should not like to offend you, but your right shoulder is much larger than your left. Obviously you are a prodigy of skill with a sabre."

"Her smile is very lovely," said Angelo to himself, "like the smile of Leonardo da Vinci's Saint John the Baptist. You do not offend me in the least," he went on aloud. "Some people have an enlarged heart. I have a distension of the right shoulder. True, it is the one I use in swordplay."

"Shall I then be labouring in vain?" asked Pauline. "What I am making for you is a jerkin to please your heart, not for fencing. You have an amazingly long arm, sir. I'll wager that without bending you could run your sword through a man lying at your horse's feet."

"I could do so, without the slightest doubt," Angelo replied, "but what need would there be to sabre a man who was already down?"

"You well know the value of insistence. We repeat litanies even to God, and would you expect the Devil to attach no importance to them? The conviction that prayers will be answered is an imperative human need. I imagine that faith holds the simplest power of healing. The most natural is always the most effective. But I should like to tell you straight away that, once you are in this tunic, you will find lavish gestures totally forbidden. These creations of mine are a sort of padded coat for men of action, but strait-jackets for men on horseback. It will allow you to pass without actual discomfort from the saddle to an armchair, but will change you from a swordsman into a cutter-out of silhouettes. You'll have just enough freedom to manipulate a pair of scissors between your thumb and index finger."

"Yet his tunic does not impede the Marquis from performing highly intricate manoeuvres on horseback. I admire him every morning as he rides across the park."

"He really does look handsome," said Pauline, "and you will be just as fine. As a matter of fact, yours will give you ample freedom."

"Thanks to your special knowledge. You have a wonderful skill in shaping these fleece jerkins to make the hips look narrow and the shoulders broad. M. le Marquis rides through the woods like Ariosto's Medor."

"You will look exactly the same. The secret lies in the little half-moon I am cutting here in the back."

"Where do you find your ideas for these designs?"

"From my fancies. Perhaps one day I will devote them to my own benefit and design a jerkin for myself," she continued after a moment of silence. "I have felt inclined to, for a long time. You have loaded me with so many compliments that now my mind is made up. The least Laurent can do is to find me four lambskins that will be just what I want. Every Medor needs an Angelica. There is enough blue paper for you and for me. Now, sir, will you, in your turn, do me the service of taking my measurements?"

Angelo was most embarrassed at having to touch her. "No approximations," she told him. "I have been scrupulously careful with your measurements, as you must be with mine. Place the tape measure straight across my shoulders. I am quite determined to look just as fine as both of you."

All this was very difficult for Angelo to do. In the end he ventured to place the tape in position, but could not avoid trembling as he did so. He smelt the exquisite perfume of her thick tresses of black hair.

"What measurement do you find? Forty centimetres?

That's what I thought. Laurent is always telling me I have shoulders like a boy. Now measure my waist."

That was a frightful moment. Angelo was obliged to drop into the nearest chair, ignoring the dictates of courtesy. Holding the tape out to Pauline, he managed to say: "I am very clumsy, and I should never forgive myself if I were to make an error that could spoil the cut of your tunic."

As he spoke he gradually recovered his spirits, in spite of the great motionless green eyes that gazed at him without wavering. "Your maid will take these measurements much more accurately than I can." He sought desperately for a phrase or two to explain his emotion, which he found quite ridiculous. Luckily it did not occur to him that he was bashful. "Until now I have lived in barracks," said he artlessly, "and you cannot imagine what a habit of brutality one has to cultivate, to govern a thousand conscripts who are their own masters at home. I am afraid of seeming boorish in the presence of such a gracious lady. That figure of forty seemed out of all reason, and has given me a terrible dread of doing something stupid with my thick fingers and this tape that I do not know how to use." Soon after he managed to find a pretext for going out, and went striding through an avenue of young elms where the icy wind did him a lot of good.

"What a boy he is!" Pauline said to herself. "One mustn't forget that he is a colonel. He did not at all like taking my measurements. He's not in the least obliging. Still, he did not try to hide it!"

All Angelo could think of was his need for intense physical exertion. He hoped it would rid him of his obscure sensation of being made to look ridiculous. "It is not possible for me to touch that woman's body," he said to himself. "How is it she does not realise that?" Nothing could have been more in tune with his state of mind than the company of those great trees as they groaned disconsolately in the wind. Though dusk was falling rapidly below thick clouds driven in from the west by the gale, he tramped far beyond the park up into the hills where, through the pine trees, he could see lights burning in that much-discussed glen where the sheepfold lay.

Strange cavalcades sometimes went out from this valley. Angelo saw one of them, one evening, passing in Indian file against the sunset. A score of mounted men emerged from the wood, crossed the clearing and made their way down through the coppice towards the road for Aix. They were all skilled riders and their horses were slender and very handsome. He heard them come galloping back in the course of the night.

"Those are my shepherds," the Marquis told him. "They sometimes go dancing at festivals. Let us go and see them."

But what he found in the glen looked nothing like a sheepfold. The building was a sort of guardhouse flanked by thick walls. "It is a Gallo-Roman sheep farm," said the Marquis. The men were practising shooting with pistols and rifles at a heap of empty bottles. "The times we read of in bucolic romances like *L'Astrée* are dead and gone," the Marquis continued. "You yourself can testify that the country is by no means peaceful. What a plum it would be for brigands to find a flock guarded only by mild dreamers! These shepherds of mine no longer have time to spend stargazing."

In the wattled enclosures, under the tall oaks, there were only about a hundred sheep. "At this time of year," the Marquis explained, "the real flock is on the seashore pastures, beyond Arles."

Pauline wanted to fire a pistol. A weapon was loaded for

her and she smashed four bottles with considerable skill. "Now it's your turn," she said to Angelo.

"This is not my speciality," Angelo replied. "I will break bottles peaceably enough, but everyone can do as much."

"And what is Monsieur's speciality?" enquired a man with the look of a sergeant.

"The sabre."

"I was gymnastic instructor in the 52nd Dragoons," said the man (he had a huge moustache and a head as round as a ball), "and I have my equipment here. Perhaps we could offer the company some entertainment?"

"Willingly," replied Angelo, thinking to himself: "Oh, well! I'll give you a good beating. Never will I sink to shooting bottles as a cure for boredom, especially in a glen where the foliage, in spite of winter, is so lovely. But when it comes to creating round my body an impenetrable lattice of steel and warming myself up in the process, I am your man."

He scorned the plastron and kept the mask pushed up over his hair like the visor of Achilles' helmet. "This thing cuts," said the sergeant, who wore a padded jacket and headguard. "You put me at a great disadvantage. I will not dare to make a stroke."

"Slash at me if you can," Angelo retorted, weaving about himself a protective curtain of three brilliantly clever flourishes. The sergeant, striking blow after blow, saved himself smartly once or twice then lowered his point. "That's enough, sir," he said. "I am no match for you. I understand that perfectly."

"A dazzling display," commented the Marquis.

"You really must teach me how to hold a sword," said Pauline.

Angelo was feeling too self-satisfied, and gave himself no time to say anything but the plain truth. Besides, he wanted to give some reassurance to the somewhat crestfallen sergeant from whom he had won such a complete victory. "If it is only a question of holding the sabre," said he "that is easy, and you need no help from me. As for wielding it, that is a man's job, and I could teach you nothing unless I treat you as a man; which will always be completely impossible. I imagine," he luckily had the grace to add, "that you do not want to learn trivialities, and one cannot learn things of value except in the heat of passion. Now, in such assaults as this, I should have to take you seriously enough to work myself up into a fury and want to cut you in pieces, which will never happen."

"Who is stopping you?" asked Pauline dryly. "I must admit," she told herself, "that he looked grand just now. No one would have cared to face him in a real fight. That little man with the big moustache was round-eyed with amazement when he began to flourish his sabre. I can well understand that such a weapon must be very tiring to the arm and calls for great physical strength. But if he would only take the trouble – I'm not asking to become a Cossack – he could very well teach me, if only a few strokes. I am sure he would really enjoy showing what he knows to a woman who interested him. God knows I don't care whether I interest him or not! But he had no need to lie." She recalled the happy phrase in which Angelo had shown the instinctive intelligence to take her seriously. "In any case, he must be given credit for not supposing it was the caprice of a frivolous woman."

All at once she blushed, turned her head aside and moved a few steps away from the others to be alone. It had just occurred to her to wonder if Angelo could have mistaken her request for an advance on her part. She recalled how spontaneously she had expressed her wish. She fancied she had even made a gesture towards him, or the hint of a gesture, and she felt such a keen pang of distress that she placed her hand over her heart.

Angelo and the Marquis, not paying the least attention to her, were testing the weight of the pistols and discussing the merit of wheel-locks. "I am lost," she said to herself. "My cursed habit of speaking freely makes me always say plainly what I want." This thought increased her mortification "Am I so base?" she wondered. "So lacking in good qualities, that I felt such a strong desire that he should teach me to use a sword?" In her guileless soul-searching, she wounded herself still more deeply. "Is that all I wanted? Did I not, in reality, want this man's company, and did I not show him as much, quite shamelessly?" A prey to this intolerable thought, she walked on a few steps and without realising it went up to a shepherd who was mending a saddle flap with a long needle and waxed thread. She stood so close to him that his jaw dropped and stood dazzled by those huge green eyes, so cold and still, that transfixed him without even seeing him. At last she gave him a little smile and turned on her heel.

One glance at Angelo completely reassured her. He, and the Marquis too, were bending over a silk handkerchief on which lay a pistol, dismantled with the point of a small knife. He was examining a spring and making it click with the point of his fingernail, gazing at it like a man inspired. Pauline was too relieved to notice Angelo's rather childish pleasure in the mechanism of a Spanish wheel. "Céline and Laurent," she said to herself, "spoke of him as a man with a passion for grandeur. Céline made fun of his largeness of spirit which struck her as ridiculous, when you remember he is not God. I have never given him any cause to despise me before today, and if I had done so just now he would not have his present air of detachment. It is obvious that nothing matters to him at the moment except that little spring he keeps buzzing with his finger."

As they were leaving, the Marquis delayed a moment to give some orders and Angelo, without a moment's thought, courteously held Pauline's stirrup for her. His mind was still dwelling upon that spring and the difference it made to the trigger release. "No," thought Pauline, "he does not think ill of me, and I did nothing wrong." She felt very happy and was the first to ride off through the coppice, at a gallop that caused both men acute anxiety.

Often the Marquis would come and spend a morning at the pavilion. He arrived in soft riding boots and a doeskin tunic, all suppleness in his leather, his body and his gestures. He had about him the air of a man keeping a watchful eye on some mystery or other. "What I like about you," he said one day, "is your integrity."

"I do not see how mine differs from other men's," Angelo replied.

"I am referring to the high standard of honour forced upon you by your constant need for grandeur."

"Nothing surprises me more than when you talk like that."

"Your surprise," replied the Marquis, "stems from the fact that you do not move in fashionable society."

"I am in your company every day," Angelo protested.

"I," the Marquis answered, "do not belong in that world, nor does my wife. That is why we get on so well together; but neither do you, and without that innate nobility of yours we should not be such good friends."

"All this" said Angelo, "seems to me totally obscure."

"A fortunate obscurity," replied the Marquis. "The fact is that one cannot doubt the truth of what you say, even when it is as extraordinary as the statement you have just this moment made. In the tone and precision of your replies there is a candour that carries all before it. You must have noticed," he went on, "that I have no liking for things that are over-emphasised. If you were to bring me a hundred proofs of your loyalty I should have grave doubts about it; with two hundred proofs, I should inevitably take you for a hypocrite; and if by some misfortune you were to persist in bringing me still more, I should not rest till I had stretched you out in some ditch or other with a nice little bullet in your brain. I possess a treasure so precious that I mean to guard it even at the peril of my friends. But your loyalty is boundless; by that I mean one cannot define its limits. There is something infinite about it that reassures me. I have carried out long experiments with men, at my own cost, and nothing disturbs me more than a loyalty within specified limits. I know it is always making excursions outside those boundaries. That is why I am talking to you with complete frankness. Here we are three human beings, unconventional in our ways to a degree that no one would believe possible. Superficial people, those, I mean, who rely on their intelligence, would calculate that from our close contact unconventional results would spring. They would not be wrong, except as to the nature of those results. For, while they are expecting them to happen within the diagram of that geometrical plane where they have verified the exactitude of the theorems they apply to the soul, those results will be accomplished in a sphere that is not only beyond their control, but beyond their comprehension."

"That makes several times," said Angelo, "that you have spoken to me in this way. I have never understood the why and wherefore or the meaning of your words."

"You could not give me clearer confirmation of my own views!" the Marquis replied. "I would not like you to think me rash. On the contrary, I flatter myself I am a prodigy of caution. It's even an example of my prudence that I tell you so."

Angelo's spirit was captivated by the beauty of the great trees in the park. They were famous, particularly a hundred or so copper beeches, the loveliest imaginable. Tortured by the winter wind, their huge branches creaked like the yards of a ship. He tried to imagine what the coming of spring would be like amid these vast stretches of rigging.

"For the first time," he said to himself, "I am thinking of a season yet to come, instead of spending my time trying to think how to act so as to live in peace with my contemporaries. Never have I known such tranquillity of spirit. That is what living really means. The man and woman who are my companions here have a way of life that enchants me. It does not call me into question. On the contrary it persuades me that I am right to be just as I am. If I had had a sister, I should have loved her to be just like this Pauline, with hair as black and a skin as white. But if my mother had had a daughter, what wouldn't she have made of her! When I was young, I always wanted a sister. If I had had one, I probably should not have thrown myself so wildly against Theresa to hide my head between her great breasts. Had she been of my own age or even younger, her very presence would have sufficed to give me every happiness, every form of courage. The corridors in the Pardi Palace are not gay at this time of year when the wind is blowing from the Alps, and one has a profound insight when one is four years old. It is perfectly natural that, after looking at the blue sky quivering outside windows pierced through walls six feet thick, I would run to nuzzle against the warm breasts of my nurse. That is why, now, old Theresa has sent me these fifty little Roman coins that I look at almost every night before I go to sleep, and that I find so moving."

One morning, Madame's chambermaid ran across the lawn and through the little birchwood, jumped across the brook and came to knock on the door of the pavilion.

Mme la Marquise begged Monsieur to come at once, if he had nothing better to do. Angelo, who had just finished shaving, smoothed his cheeks with the back of his hand, took up the razor again and scraped a little more at the corners of his mouth and round his chin. Before going in to see Pauline he examined his boots. They were in perfect order. Pauline looked troubled. She was extremely kind, but her cordiality was plainly forced. She cleared the armchair that stood near her, then the chaise-longue, then a pouffe. Her hands were full of sewing things, linen, pincushions, workbaskets, and she said to him: "Sit down," but he felt that she did not in the least want him to sit. She could not conceal the fact that, if she had had the power to make him vanish in a puff of smoke, she would have done so on the instant without remorse, and smiled afterwards. At last she did smile. "Will you do something to please me?" she asked.

There was a long silence. "Yes," said Angelo. He did not know what to think and was very uneasy.

"Now that the weather is better," said Pauline, "I go every morning to walk at the edge of the pond. Have you never seen me?"

"No," Angelo replied. "The willow buds are out now, and they make a green mist that still prevents my being able to see the opposite bank."

"It is to your side of the lake that I come," said Pauline, "and sometimes I am no more than a few yards from your window. Besides, I usually wear this wide crimson gown that I have on at this moment, and such a vivid red ought to be noticed, even through a cloud of little willow catkins."

Angelo was so disconcerted by the tone of this conversation, said to be important and preceded by such visible signs of emotion, that he could think of no reply beyond a banal phrase or two. "If I did see your dress," he said, "you were far from my thoughts and I must have imagined it was a bush in flower."

"There is no need to say gallant things to me," Pauline replied severely, "and in any case there is not a single flowering shrub known that has blossoms of this shade of red. Look at my dress properly, and you must agree that is so. You did not see me, that's plain. Do not try to make excuses. It is very natural. Now I clearly understand that air of profound indifference you have when you walk to and fro in your room. For I have certainly seen you, several times. I have even heard you, and that is why I asked you to come here this morning."

She still retained her air of severity and Angelo wondered what she could have heard. "Did I swear? That's very unlikely if I was looking profoundly indifferent. I never swear at such times."

"You whistle very well," Pauline continued.

"Ah, yes! I do whistle," Angelo agreed with a fatuous little smile. He was growing irritated by all these mysteries and was well aware they were making him look ridiculous. "I cannot sing, so I have learned to whistle the music I like for my own pleasure. Did that annoy you?"

"On the contrary," said Pauline. "I took great pleasure listening to a little Mozart and a little Cimarosa that I did not know very well. But I also heard you whistle a piece by Brahms that I do know and love. It is called *Regrets*. Now, you do not whistle it correctly, and that is very irritating to anyone who attaches a sentimental value to those phrases. The opening passage is quite right, so is the last, but you make several bad mistakes in the delicate sequence that carries on the melody in between. Or, more accurately, you improvise. Now, as I have just told you, I have already lost my heart to the music as Brahms wrote it, and as I will play it on the piano for you in a moment. Try to learn it, in case you might like to whistle *Regrets* on some other occasion when the red of my dress clashes with your willow buds." She opened the lid of the piano and set to playing the Brahms.

Angelo was wild with anger. All this had been said in a cold, stern tone, and not once did her big green eyes show a spark of animation. "I have a perfect right to whistle what I like as I like," he thought to himself. "And you are not the first to attach a sentimental value to that melody. It spoke to my heart and brought me to tears when you were no more than a baby crying for your milk. When I asked Anna's musicians to play *Regrets*, it was to bring my mother to my mind's eye, as she sat at the piano in front of the great window that looks out over a hundred leagues of the Alps. I was seven, then, and the same height standing as she was when seated. 'Rest your cheek against my shoulder, Angelo,' she would say, 'my little angel from heaven.'"

Pauline played the Brahms with sensitive appreciation. Her dress, of crimson with a touch of gold, half-covered her shoulders and fitted closely over her bust, but billowed around her hips. "She is very lovely," mused Angelo. "There is a sadness in her glance – doubtless that is why I do not like green eyes," he thought abruptly – "but, when she was talking to me so sternly just now her mouth was poised very sweetly in her narrow cheeks, and at this moment, as I gaze at her snowy nape and her lovely black hair, I feel as distracted as Perceval when he saw the blood of wild geese against the snow."

He did not notice that Pauline, after playing the melody perfectly, was now, very discourteously, repeating with some insistence the passage she had spoken of. At last she closed the piano, and Angelo rose to his feet. "It is true," he said coldly, "that I did improvise a little here and there, but that will never happen again since I have just learned the phrases that were missing. I am sure you will have the greatest indulgence for my past mistakes when I tell you that this music (which has a great sentimental importance for me as well as for you) is linked with a period of despair in my mother's life. I was seven, then, and she would make me lean my cheek against her shoulder as she played. I paid more attention to drying her tears than to learning the precise notes. Beyond question, a sensitive child, hearing that opening passage at such a time, could never forget it. As for the rest, which I improvised so that I might the longer enjoy my memories of that adorable woman who is the great love of my life, I would ask you to be good enough to notice that, if I made mistakes in what you call the *nuances*, I nevertheless composed the concluding passage exactly as Brahms himself did. I am very proud of that." He smiled, bowed and went out.

"I never succeed in doing what I set out to do," said Pauline to herself. "Why did he look so cross. Yet I took care to remain very serious, as I promised myself I would. He ought to have understood that since we are friends I attach a great deal of importance to everything he does, and especially to what goes on in his heart when he is alone in that isolated little pavilion beside the lake.

"I wonder what he would have done if I had adopted the air of supreme indifference he had as he stood by his window while I was among the willows, where it was impossible for him not to see me in this dress, the most colourful one I have."

"We must look carefully among the willows," Angelo reminded himself. "Spring is passing quickly and making them thicker every day. But I have good eyes, and there is certainly no red dress among them now."

One lovely calm night, when all the nightingales were singing in the great beech trees motionless, now, and full of leaves – Angelo fancied he saw a white veil on the far side of the pool. He had not yet lit his lamp. "She will not be able to accuse me of indifference," he said to himself. "From over there, I doubt if she can even see the black outline of my little window in the pavilion wall." Very beautifully, he whistled *Regrets*. The patch of white did not stir from its patch of grass. Angelo watched it for more than an hour before he realised that it was the foliage of a little aspen.

"I am as stupid as a cabbage," he told himself. "What sense is there in trying to get my own back? Let's settle it by agreeing that Pauline would make an adorable sister. The only one I should like to have. Since I have her, why be so mean? That fancy she had for summoning me in mid-morning and receiving me so haughtily in her crimson gown to point out to me the notes I had forgotten in a German melody – all that is exactly the sort of thing my mother might have done. Why didn't I notice that at once? I shall be forgetting my way about the Pardi Palace next! I must beware! My spirit is growing fat and lazy!"

The weather was beginning to be very hot at times. Often the south lay open for days on end to the wind from Africa bringing gusts of stifling air and scuds of rain. Then through the endless hours of daylight a pale copper-coloured glow rolled over the hills.

On the look-out for the crimson gown, Angelo caught sight of a lavender-blue dress that sometimes skirted the edge of a clump of cypress trees and made its way up towards the terraced olive groves on the slope where the hermitage stood. With swift little steps he ran in that direction, making a wide detour, and finally paused to stroll among the hollows where lush beds of spearmint grew in amazing profusion. He watched the dress go up to the little chapel and remain there for some time fluttering in the porch. At last it decided to come back down, moving straight towards the low ground where the mint beds lay. Then he slipped into a little gully hidden by arbutus, and began to jump from stone to stone across the rushes of a marsh till he reached the banked edge of a canal. Now he was sure it was Pauline, swaying as she walked along the water's brink. He could clearly see her thick black hair and the white flesh of her neck and shoulders. In all probability if the lavender-blue dress continued to follow the canal, its wearer would not be able to resist the impulse to walk over the aqueduct, as all little girls like to do. Angelo strode, very quickly this time, along a sunken path covered with flowering hawthorn, but when he arrived at the aqueduct the blue dress was already making its way back to the chateau across the wide lawns.

There was a heavy storm; then two or three more that were very beautiful to watch. Lightning struck the pine wood on the slopes of the Vauvenargues. Pauline loved these dramas. But she said to herself: "What point is there in climbing the hill to see? The flames must be red, the smoke black, and the fire must take the course it always does along the flank of the Sauvan where the pine trees are so dry. At last I have reached the stage of being sufficient unto myself. Never have I known such a peace of mind. I ought to rearrange this room and make it more charming. What it needs more than anything else is some screens. To make little hiding places, so that one never has far to run from one little secret haven to the next. Mask the windows as much as possible; nothing is more tiresome than a wide view. At heart, what I like least of all is space. I should like the very opposite: something quite tiny and secure, like a nest."

Angelo was thinking: "I seem to have reached the same point as I did before. I need friends. I would give ten years of my life for another look at those fervent eyes of my friend, the engineer from the Tyrol. Who knows whether it would not have been wisdom to accept his foreman's job? I miss the companionship of those loyal, passionate souls. For certain, if I were working in the yards beside them they would make me one of themselves and love me. Then there is some flavour in what one does."

He went down to the village. "I wonder," he thought "what has happened to that cheeky coachman, the one with whom I almost had a fight and who later greeted me like a soldier at the inn? He seemed to me the sort of man I could get on with. The Marquis is a model of rectitude but with him I always have the impression of being about to fight a duel." He went into the inn, where he was given a rather awkward business-like smile of welcome. The landlord, who was driving away flies with a duster, did not interrupt this activity. "If *M. le Colonel* had let me know he was coming," said the man, who was obviously uneasy, "I would have had the room shaded and the courtyard watered."

"This is not what I want," thought Angelo. "To the devil with these 'colonels' and arrangements made in advance. What I need is friendliness, to have someone beside me who will make me feel complete. What a pity this black-haired woman is so cantankerous, or, rather, that she has no need of friendship. If she were my sister, everything would be fine!"

"Tonight you are on guard," the Marquis told him. "I have to go with my shepherds to a festival, partly religious, partly veterinary, that is taking place in the hills around Sainte-Baume, beyond Saint-Maximin. To miss it would be to offer a slight to a great many powers that be, not least to my shepherds themselves. They will soon be leaving for the Alps, and I am, after all, very concerned that the lambing season shall be fruitful and well supervised. We must be careful to ensure that gods and men are on our side. But that will compel me to spend half the night out of doors. Will you come and stay with my wife this evening, till I return? I do not like to leave her alone, once summer has come. The woods are full of tramps, and here we always leave our doors open to benefit from any wind. Not that Pauline would be incapable of defending herself unaided. She certainly can, and it may well be that she even enjoys doing so. But an intruder would not know that, and she would be obliged to teach him by stretching him out stone dead. Now, as it happens, I do not want any corpses around. In the ordinary way they would not worry me, for the servants sweep the place every morning. But at this particular time I am a little bit touchy on that score."

Angelo waited until the dusk was far advanced, then went with short, quick steps to the chateau. "Why are you so late?" asked Pauline.

"I knew you were well able to defend yourself without any help. And, moreover, for the last two hours I have been on the alert, ready to run over at the least sign of disturbance."

"Of course I can protect myself, as you say, just as I could have eaten, by myself, these junkets and preserves, but I chose to wait for you."

They settled themselves in front of the French window opening on to the terrace, and, little by little, night fell. Though only the table stood between them, they could no longer see each other: the great beech trees made the darkness more intense.

"I am happy," said Pauline.

"I am completely happy, too," Angelo replied.

"There is not the slightest wind," she said. "The beeches are so still that they seem like sculptured trees. One no longer needs to see; simply by listening to them one knows just where the nightingales are, whether they are beside each other or spaced at intervals far into the distance."

"Do you often have such periods of calm here?" Angelo asked.

"Never. This is the very first time it has been quiet enough for me to hear the profound peace of the country. It is magnificent."

"I have never felt such a sense of utter rest."

"And of fulfilment. Never have I had as many things to enjoy as I have tonight. I can hear foxes barking far away, in a spot that, by day, seems only a handful of blue mist merging with the sky. How wonderful to grow richer and richer without stirring a single step."

"I did not think such a thing was possible," said Angelo.

"I quite expected it," she replied.

"A terrifying calm."

"But full of healing."

"Amazingly so. I should like to go away, one of these days."

"To go where?"

"To look for adventure. One needs to go on seeking."

"Are you not satisfied here?" asked Pauline.

"This is exactly what I need to find," said Angelo. "If only this happiness could endure!"

"There is no reason why it should not last," Pauline replied. "It depends only on ourselves."

"Do you really think it rests with us?"

"And do you really think the world can be so different tonight from what it was last night?" she asked.

"I know," said Angelo, "that the world is what we make it."

"Then," said Pauline, "what adventures do you seek, other than what we have succeeded in finding this very evening? If this is what you are really looking for."

"Upon my soul," said Angelo, "I desire nothing more."

"Five minutes ago, we thought that nothing could be lovelier, and, you see, things have grown more beautiful every moment. Can you not hear, now, noises still further away than the barking of the foxes we heard a minute ago? It seems like a sort of light that can express itself without needing to destroy the darkness."

"For the first time in my life," said Angelo, "I desire nothing more than what I have."

"I will have the lamps lit," said Pauline. "Let us try to go very quietly to the great salon and stay there a while."

"That is the most terrifying adventure I could possibly undertake."

"A little confidence is all you need," she assured him. "Give me your hand, and let us walk slowly. Come."

The lamps were already lit. Pauline imposed silence, her finger to her lip. She seated herself and took up some needlework that lay ready to hand upon a little table. "Really it would look better if I were darning socks," she said in a low voice. "Take a book and read. We had better not talk any more." Angelo took a seat ten steps away from her.

"What reason have I for being so happy?" he wondered. "It is not the calm of the night, for the happiness I know now is even greater than it was a few moments ago." He opened a book, but did not read. He had no desire to smoke. He had never seen anything lovelier than what lay now before his eyes. He held a volume of the *Magasin pittoresque* and Pauline was busy with her lacemaking.

At last it struck midnight. Angelo noticed a movement of the window curtain. He turned his head. The door was open and on the threshold the Marquis stood looking at them. He must have been there for a moment or two already. "Terribly sorry to disturb such peace," he said.

* * *

Immediately after dawn, a knock fell on the door of the pavilion. It was the Marquis. His face looked tired. "Have you not slept?" Angelo asked him.

"I am in pain, a little," the Marquis replied, "but Pauline has attended to me perfectly. You must do me a service. Dress, saddle a horse, and leave at once. I want you to take a letter for me. I have no wish to gild the pill for you; it is possible that, after last night's affair, certain persons may be very anxious to intercept the letters I do not send by post."

"Explain nothing," said Angelo, and on the instant he made ready to start.

Also by Jean Giono

THE HORSEMAN ON THE ROOF
Translated by Jonathan Griffin

A swashbuckling story set in Provence in the early nineteenth century, during the great cholera epidemic.

"Fantastical and episodic, the reason why this novel exerts such a hold on the reader is rooted in Giono's brilliant, unaffected powers of description"   SOPHIA SACKVILLE-WEST, *Standard*

"The sensuousness of Giono's prose captures the white heat and oppressive atmosphere of the Provençal countryside"
JULIA REID, *Scotsman*

"A fabulously sensual writer"   HELEN STEVENSON, *The Times*

"Giono's naturalistic prose has a hypnotic quality that is at its most impressive when he is describing the wild beauty and grandeur of the Provençal landscape"   EUAN CAMERON, *Daily Telegraph*

"These images of Provence have a hypnotic violence akin to Van Gogh at his most vivid, but Giono also provides a great story, not least one of love"   DAVID HUGHES, *Mail on Sunday*

"Giono's book seems like a giant tapestry of its terrain and time"
DEREK MALCOLM, *Guardian*